# *The*
# SELLAMILLION

# *The* SELLAMILLION

# A. R. R. R. ROBERTS

GOLLANCZ
LONDON

Copyright © A. R. R. R. Roberts 2004
*All rights reserved*

The right of Adam Roberts to be identified as the
author of this work has been asserted by him in accordance
with the Copyright, Designs and Patents Act 1988.

First published in Great Britain in 2004 by
Gollancz
An imprint of the Orion Publishing Group
Orion House, 5 Upper St Martin's Lane,
London WC2H 9EA

A CIP catalogue record for this book is
available from the British Library

ISBN 0 575 07611 9

Typeset at The Spartan Press Ltd,
Lymington, Hants

Printed in Great Britain by
Clays Ltd, St Ives plc

www.orionbooks.co.uk

# CONTENTS

## Ainusoul: the Music of the Ainu

# The Sellamillion: The History of the Sellāmi

# The History of the War of the Thing™

# Appendices

# The Sellamillion
## An Introduction, by B C D 'Pierrre' Roberts

My grand-uncle A. R. R. Roberts has achieved a globally world-wide famousness the world over for his celebrated Heroic Fighting Fantasy masterpieces: *The Soddit*, *Lowered off the Rings* and *Farmer Giles of Yokel-Caricature*. Now sadly deceased or 'passed on' as he himself put it, it falls to me to collect together his uncollected Fantasy writings and offer to the public these valuable sketches, designs, memoirs and other writings under the general title *The Sellamillion*.

### 1. Life

My grand-uncle's full name was 'Adam Robinson? Robertson? Robins? ah, Roberts I See Do Excuse Me I'm Dreadfully Sorry I Left My Spectacles In The Vestry', which is how the Rev. Roland Adorno baptised him, reading from a chit given him by the organist. It was this full version of his name that was, for legal reasons, entered on the birth certificate. Accordingly, and although my grand-uncle was known to his myriad fans by the abbreviated form of his name, the full surname was required for all official arenae.[1]

His career at the University of Oxoford, where he sat in the Ikea Chair of Dead and Terminally Ill Languages, was lengthy and successful. He distinguished himself as a scholar and also as a member of the group known as 'the oinklings', the celebrated pork-themed writers' group, who met Thursdays throughout term to discuss their various literary productions over bacon and chops.

## 2. Two Robertses's?

It is sometimes said, with some justification, that there were actually two A. R. R. R. Robertses: A. R. R. R. Roberts, the noted and bestselling fantasy author, and Professor Roberts I See Do Excuse Me I'm Dreadfully Sorry I Left My Spectacles In The Vestry, the Oxford scholar. Indeed, my granduncle himself declared that he was 'split' or 'divided'

---

1 This I take to be the plural of *arena*. Although, actually, when I look at it written down like that, it may be that 'arena' is *already* the plural of 'arenum.' Is that right? If it is, then that would make 'arenae' the plural plural of arenum. I don't mind admitting I'm nervous – it's no easy thing writing an introduction to a collection of writings by a world-class philologist and grammatologist. I could so easily make a fool of myself. I'm anxious to get the grammar and such just so.

after this fashion. 'There are two of me,' he told the *Oxford Times* in an interview late in his career. 'The writer and the academic. Both, luckily, are called Roberts, and at the moment both live in the same town. It has not always been arranged so neatly. Two years ago the two were Geoff Kapitza, a Shrewsbury-based supplier of industrial ceramics, and Susan Eley, the author with David Blackbourn of *The Peculiarities of German History*. That was a rather awkward set-up, I don't mind telling you.'

As one illustration of the sort of life my grand-uncle lived in the ivied halls and hallowed ives[2] of Ballsiol College, Oxford, I append this record of a conversation he had with his distinguished colleague Professor Sir Algernon Islwyn De Vere Hedgecock Twistleton Faineant Mainwaring Featherstonehaugh Jones. In common with many of the Fellows of Ballsiol, Professor Jones frequently congratulated my grand-uncle on what he considered a properly and unashamedly-hyphenated Traditional English surname. [The following excerpt is from *Porter! A Porter's Life*, by Henry Porter, Porter of Saint Peter Hall, Oxford]

---

2  This should be 'eaves'.

I was sitting [writes Porter] in the Porter's box at Saint Peter's, drinking some Port and reading a local historical account of Portsmouth, when Professor A. R. R. R. Roberts entered the college, visiting a friend. In the course of his ingress he happened to bump into Professor Jones, who was exiting. 'Well,' cried Professor Jones, warmly, 'if it isn't my good friend Professor Roberts I See Do Excuse Me I'm Dreadfully Sorry I Left My Spectacles In The Vestry. A very good evening, *anima dimidia mea.*'

'My dear Professor Sir Algernon Islwyn De Vere Hedgecock Twistleton Faineant Mainwaring Featherstonehaugh Jones,' replied Professor Roberts, genially, 'how wonderful to see you.'

Professor Jones's face fell.

'My dear Professor Roberts I See Do Excuse Me I'm Dreadfully Sorry I Left My Spectacles In The Vestry,' he expostulated. 'I fear I must correct you – it is pronounced "fanshaw".'

Professor Roberts naturally looked abashed. 'I am sorry, my friend. I thought I had pronounced it "fanshaw".'

'You did indeed pronounce the penultimate element of my surname "fanshaw" and most correctly. But you mispronounced the earlier element – it is pronounced "fanshaw", and not "hedge-cock" as *you* said.'

'I cannot apologise enough,' declared Professor Roberts. 'Allow me to address you again, my dear Professor Sir Algernon Islwyn De Vere Hedgecock Twistleton Faineant Mainwaring Featherstonehaugh Jones, in the hope of correcting my grievous error.'

Professor Jones shook his head. 'No, no,' he said. 'This time you got the first "fanshaw" right but monkeyed up the second one.'

'I did? I said "fanshaw", didn't I?'

'You said "farnshow"; quite, quite wrong.'

'Professor Sir Algernon Islwyn De Vere Hedgecock Twistleton Faineant—'

'No, no,' interrupted Professor Jones, becoming heated. 'Faineant isn't "fayno", as you say it, it is pronounced *"fanshaw"*. Must I write it down in phonetic script?'

'There is no need to be offensive,' retorted Professor Roberts, bridling.

'I'll be offensive if I choose,' returned Professor Jones, hotly.

'A figo,' said Professor Roberts.

'A figo for *you*, sir.'

The two professors were forever falling out with one another in this fashion.

### 3. The Soddit

My grand-uncle first wrote his children's classic *The Soddit* on the back (and later, when he ran out of space, on the front in thick black felt-tip) of certain student examination papers he was supposed to be marking. After its publication and unexpected success, his publishers pressed him for a sequel. As he wrote to his dear friend C John Lewis:

> My publishers pressed me for a sequel again yesterday. I do wish they'd stop doing that. Always pressing, poking, can't keep their hands to themselves. 'We'll keep on doing this,' Stanley Nonwin told me, pressing a tender spot near my spleen, 'until you deliver the sequel, you little jerk.' Or at least that's what I think he said. His editorial assistant, Hefty Jill, was sitting on my head and had my arms in a three-quarter nelson at the time. I fear I shall have to oblige them.

His three-volume gymnasium-set fantasy, *Lowered Off the Rings*, was written during the war, and published to great acclaim on both sides of the Atlantic. The acclaim was, as it happens, for a different book: *Brass Rubbing* by Juliana Nederlandia. But as Nonwin told my grand-uncle 'That's not the important thing – the important thing is that there is acclaim sloshing about. It creates the right sort of atmosphere into which to release a new book – means that people are favourably disposed towards books in general, you see.'

Nonwin's optimism was duly rewarded when *Lowered Off the Rings* became a Hot Hundred Bestseller-List-Chaser Likely-to-Sell title in the *Midlands Advertiser* 'What's Up in Books?' supplement. With great sales came great fame. 'I find,' my grand-uncle wrote to his friend Lewis, 'that I am famous. It is not fanciful to say so. The fanfaronade of fandom treats me with frightening familiarity.'

### 4. The Sellamillion

The world created by A. R. R. Roberts was no mere fantasy flimflam or flapdoodle, believe you me. It was fully rounded, no, wait a mo, that doesn't roll off the tongue right, not the fully rounded, that's fine, the bit before. 'Believe you me'. I'm not sure that that sounds right. Hmm, hm, um, how about, 'You believe me'? Maybe that's better. Or, even, 'Believe me, you!' Yes, that's the best one. Vocative case. I say, Miriam, when you transcribe this bit into your word processor, could you please cut out my dithering and so on? Just cut straight to the – yes, right. Thanks.

So, hem, yes, Upper Middle Earth, no flapdoodle, on the contrary, where was I, yes – it was a lifetime's work; a detailed land of many nations and languages. The present volume assembles the background myths and stories to the *Soddit* and to *Lowered Off the Rings* as well as much alternate material, early drafts, and the like. By the way Miriam, that's a lovely chemise. No, really, a very nice purple.

The volume includes material relating to the 'singing' of the cosmos into being by the Ainu, the 'souls' or divine subordinates of the Creator, as well as the History of the Sellāmi, a magical artefact stolen from the Undying Lands. Certain elements relating to the War of the Thing™ that also formed the basis of the *Lowered Off the Rings* trilogy.

Well, enough of my yakking! No, on second thoughts, Miriam, don't put that, put something conventional like 'I will not weary the reader with lengthy preliminaries, et cetera et cetera'. Oh, and we'd better say that we're using some of the letters that C John Lewis exchanged with grand-uncle as a sort of preface to the volume. In addition to this preface. A postpreface preface. Post-preface, but pre the, um, face of the main text.

I'd like to thank my three research assistants, who

have worked tirelessly helping me assemble this collection of disparate material: Gabriel Kay, Guy Bedevere and Adrian Ladyofthelake.

## Some letters between A. R. R. R. Roberts and C John Lewis
## The Genesis of the Sellamillion

Cedric John Lewis was perhaps the most famous of my grand-uncle's many friends. He has, of course, subsequently gained worldwide celebrity as the author of a Fantasy sequence of his own – the 'Nerdia' books: a series of children's fantasy adventures about two boys and two girls who clamber, with some difficulty, through a magic sock-drawer in an interdimensional wardrobe, thence into the magic kingdom of Nerdia where they meet the gentle though dispute-prone Lion Aslef and the Wicked Queen Feminist, who is evil, wrong, misguided and I-want-my-supper-on-t'table-when-I-get-in. Not all admirers of these books realise (so cunningly and cleverly did the author conceal his spiritual aim) that Lewis wrote them as allegories to express and prose-lytise his own religious faith, with Aslef representing The Christ. The books in the sequence are: Volume 1, *The Passion Of The Lion, The Wicked Jews Who Murdered Him, and The Wardrobe*; Volume 2, *The Boy*

*And His Horse And The Unspeakable Immorality They Got Up To Together Because They Did Not Attend Properly To The Commands of Leviticus*; Volume 3, *The Voyage Of The Duty To Tread down Upon Heretics*; Volume 4, *HIV Is God's Plague On The Immoral* and the final volume, *Worship My God Ye Infidels Or You Will All Burn Forever*. He, and the other members of the 'oinklings', corresponded extensively with my grand-uncle during the composition of his Fantasy writings; and from this extensive correspondence I have selected a few letters that cast, I think, an interesting light on the production of the *Sellamillion* itself.

My dear AR

I'd be very grateful if you'd let me know your opinion of the following, which I found in the Library's Casanova MSS archive yesterday. I hope to include it in my forthcoming *Venetian Jokes*:[3]

> —*I say I say I say, my Doge has no nose.*
> —*No nose? How does he smell?*
> —*Lacking a nose he cannot smell at all, which is if anything a boon when we consider the notoriously unpleasant odour associated with the Venetian canals.*

By the way, how's your Fantasy epic proceeding?
Best wishes,
C


Dear C John

Thank you for the joke. Very droll.

I'm glad you ask about the Fantasy epic. I confess I'm having a spot of bother with Nonwin about the

---

3   Lewis's *Venetian Jokes* was eventually published by the Oxford Open Press Syndicate in four volumes under the title *Parlo Parlo Parlo: the Jokes of Venice*. Unfortunately, Lewis's policy of translating not only the jokes but also the surnames of the original creators of the jokes led to difficulties when an over-zealous copyeditor overapplied the system. Lewis wanted the name of the celebrated lover 'Giacomo Casanova' rendered as 'Jack Newhouse'; but in the first edition it was instead rendered throughout as 'Fuckall Barrethome'. The entire print run had to be pulped.

follow-up to the *Soddit* and *Lowered Off the Rings*. He wants another of the same stamp, and won't take no for an answer. Worse than that, he won't take 'yes, in a year or two' for an answer either. I tried explaining to him that the conventions of academic publishing permit an author a dozen years to assemble material and another seven to write it up, but he spoke scornful words in reply.

Apparently the marketing department has a slot with the *Fantasy Book Club – Not So Much A Club, More Thor's Hammer!!* (I give you the exact title of this organisation, down to the last exclamation mark) for February, and the sequel must be ready by then. What am I to do? My imagination is utterly mined out and exhausted. What shall I do?

Warmest regards, A

Dear AR
I advise prayer. In fact, I've just published the enclosed little book, *The Joy of Grace and the Gracefulness of Joy*, with Christian Publishing Inc. I make so bold as to send you a copy in the hope that it is of some devotional use. In particular, I'd like to direct your attention to Chapter 5 *Those Who Say 'Christ' instead of 'The Christ' Will Go To Hell For Evermore* and Chapter 11 *God Was A Carpenter, which*

*means that All Articles of Woodwork and/or Furniture Are Sacred, Therefore Anybody Defacing, Denting Or Mistreating Woodwork Will Go To Hell For Evermore*. I hope it is of some use in your dealings with your publisher.

    Best Wishes,

    CJL

Dear Lewis

Thank you for the book, which I shall read at my earliest opportunity. I note with particular pleasure the topic of Chapter 14, *God Created Man in His Image, but Some Men Look* Exactly *Like Monkeys For Crying Out Loud, Hairy Knuckle-Dragging Weirdos That They Are: a Paradox in the Conflict Between Christianity and Darwinism Addressed*. It is about time somebody got to the bottom of that particular theological conundrum.

    Here's news: I've just had the strangest conversation, on the High Street. To be honest I'm not sure what to make of it. I was walking along on my way to college this morning when I was stopped by a tall, handsome blonde-haired chap wearing plenty of velvet and a monocle. He said 'excuse me,' and was most polite throughout; but he insisted that he had read my published Fantasy books and they were 'often wrong'. He added that I had done very well, by and large; but that there were certain crucial errors in the text.

I demurred, obviously; and suggested that I might be permitted a little leeway with my own fictional inventions – hoping to imply that, as author of these fantasies, *I* can hardly be 'wrong'. At this he gave me a very strange look, and thrust into my hand a sheaf of unbound manuscript. 'You'll perhaps find the following notes I have made on the genuine mythology of interest,' he said. I thanked him and tried to decline the gift, but he wouldn't take the papers back. When I asked to whom I owed thanks for this unusual gift, he replied that his name was Terry (I think), and that 'no thanks were necessary' beyond the correction of certain misapprehensions about the nature of Upper Middle Earth. Then he said goodbye, linked arms with a beautiful but vacant-looking young woman, and walked away.

And do you know the strangest thing of all? The beautiful young woman with whom he departed had *only one hand*. Is that not strange?

Better go and look at this manuscript. Best wishes,

A

## Part 1
# Ainusoul: the Music of the Ainu

[*Editor's Note*: the 'Ainusoul' was the earliest element in my grand-uncle's personal mythology, dealing as it does with the creation of Upper Middle Earth, the coming of Evil into that world, the creation of elves and various other things. It is, strictly, a separate thing from the 'Sellamillion' proper, which concerns that magic artefact known as the Sellāmi. I print the 'Ainusoul' here in six sections, beginning with the first. Obviously. It exists in a remarkably finished form, perhaps the result of many separate processes of revision and polishing; the contrast with the later material in the 'Sellamillion' is very noticeable. Well, I noticed it anyway. And you will notice it too. I mean, if you want to. I'm not instructing you to notice it or anything. Only if you feel like it. Really, it's up to you.]

## The Creation

In the beginning, 'twas *Emu*, or *Ainu*, the one, that in Asdar is called *Rhodhulsarm*, and verily he 'twas, was rather, for he was without form and escheweth the vacancy *of* Chaos. Yea, verily, even *unto* the vacancy thereof. And He *did* call in veritude with Furious Wrath and a Mighty Wind, which did *Blow Mightily*, and He did Summon with Wormwood *and* Gall the *Cornet, Flute, Harp, Sackbut, Psaltery, Dulcimer* and a really pretty quite impressive variety of brazen instrumentation, actually. Then sayeth *Emu*, 'Behold! I shall Spew Ye From My Belly *and* Devour you thereof, and cry in a big voice.' And the Holy Spirits that are called Valūpac, gathered about Emu and their names are Gion, Poll, Gorge, Thingo, and Moregothic. And the Creations of Emu, the holy souls called Valūpac, sayeth, 'What Shall ye Cry?' And He replieth *to them*, 'He that diggeth a pit shall fall into the darkness thereof. A bundle of Myrrh is he who smiteth me, with the gnashing of teeth and the wailing of flutes from the bowels of wailing and the chins of gnashing. For how agree the kettle

3

and the earthen pot together? Yea, verily, *even* unto the agreeing thereof.'

And his Creations said to Emu, 'Do what?'

And Emu said, 'Didn't I just explain it?'

And the Holy Spirits did reply, 'Yeah, great, great, what was the, er, middle bit again?'

And Emu said, 'Just sing. I'm going to sing the cosmos into being and your job is to sing backing vocals. OK?'

And the Holy Spirits replied 'Ahh' in tones of dawning comprehension.

And so they sang.

But one Spirit among the Backing Singers of Emu was not pleased with the harmony, and this was Moregothic. He said, 'What's all this then? Are we just going to be singing all through eternity, is it? Can't we have a breather, maybe a drink?'

And Emu said, 'Just get on with the baritone line, for crying out loud, you're spoiling the close harmony.'

And Moregothic said, 'My throat is hurting.'

And Emu said, 'Well that's your own fault, now, isn't it? I told you, sing from the chest, from the chest, *laaa!* like that, not the throat, you'll be giving yourself polyps if you're not careful. And if you do, don't say I didn't warn you, don't come crying to me, or croaking, don't come croaking to me if that's what happens.'

And Moregothic said, 'So, just out of curiosity, really, I'm wondering why an all-seeing, omniscient and all-powerful God of Goodness would allow something like oesophageal polyps to develop in the first place?'

And Emu, colouring a little, said, 'That's just part of my ineffability, isn't it?'

And Moregothic said, 'You what?'

And Emu repeated, in a tight voice, 'My ineffability.'

And Moregothic, though he seemed to be nodding in agreement with this Divine pronouncement of the ultimate mysterious and transcendental unknowability of God's Will, yet he said under his breath, 'No effing ability, more like.'

And Emu said, 'I heard that! I heard that, that's no way to talk to your Supreme Being and, I might add, Creator, though I've got no thanks off any of you for that. Just a couple of words, thank you never hurt anyone, gave you the best years of my omnipotence and this is how I'm repaid.'

And Moregothic said, 'Well if you're going to be like that, I'm off.'

And Emu said, 'Well, go off then, see if I care.'

And Moregothic said, 'I will.'

And Emu said, 'Go ahead then.'

And Moregothic said, 'I will.'

And Emu said, 'I'm all-powerful, I could create a million more Backing Singers for my song if I wanted to.'

And Moregothic said, 'If you're so all-powerful, how could it be that you've mistaken me for somebody who gives a toss?'

And so it was that the great cleavage occurred between the Almighty Emu and the Dark Lord Moregothic.

## Of the Coming of the Elves and the First Wars of Good Against Evil

So it was that Moregothic fled the realm of Asdar and came to Upper Middle Earth. And Upper Middle Earth had been sung into existence by Emu and his subsidiary spirits, the Valūpac, and accordingly it wasn't terribly well defined – very beautiful, I'm not denying that, lovely in a sort of haunting way, but not very *precise*, if you see what I mean. Lots of mist, a bit of sky, but when you tried to pick out specifics it all sort of blended in. A bit melty ice-creamy, if you know what I mean. A little bit too much late Monet. Cotton-woolly. Candy-flossy. You get the picture.

And Moregothic said, 'Blimey, this is something of a bodge job, isn't it?'

And he realised he was talking to himself.

So Moregothic made for himself followers. He took the earth of Upper Middle Earth (the earth after which the land was, I suppose, named); and because it was only song and without words, it could be

impressed with a great many different inter-
pretations; and so Moregothic did create creations
with it. Creatures, I suppose you could call them,
which is, I suppose, where that word comes from.
That had never really occurred to me before.

First he created four dragons. First, he made the
Dragon of the East, who was a league from snout to
tail, with blazing golden scales and scarlet eyes. And
he made the Dragon of the West, whose skin was
blemishless and blue-purple, and whose eyes were
bright with the silver of the evening star. And he
made the Dragon of the North, who was ice-white,
with breath that chilled and claws that shattered the
strongest metal. And at the last he made the Dragon
of the South, who was wine-coloured with olive-
coloured eyes, and wings as wide as stormclouds;
and his nostrils shed lightning upon the sky that fell
in thorn-shapes through the darkening air. And
these four mighty dragons reared from the dust in
glory.

And Moregothic had brought over from Asdar one
of the junior Valūpac, who had elected to rebel
against Emu, and to share in the labours and share
in the triumph of Moregothic. And this being was
called *Sharon*, for nobody seemed to realise that this

was a girl's name. And Moregothic made him his lieutenant.[4]

And then he blew his breath into a fistful of earth, or something along those lines, and created a mighty army of evil creatures, that he called Orks. He intended fully to call them Awe-Inspiring Warriors of Darkness, but breathing in to speak this terrible name a fragment of dust flew up his nose, causing him to half-cough, half-snort, and so they were ever after known by that noise.

Now, the four great dragons were the mightiest of Moregothic's creations; and their being contained the greatest proportion of the earth of Upper Middle Earth and the smallest proportion of the breath of Moregothic; and ever after they were the least bound to his will, the most ornery and independent. And the Orks were the least part fragments and motes of dust from the original matter of Emu's song, and were the largest part breath and spittle of Moregothic, and they were the most bound to his will and the evilest.

The Dragons took wing and flew. But they found

---

4    You, dear reader, must decide whether you intend to pronounce this word in the manner of the forces of Good and Light and Reason and Decency, as Emu does himself, 'luptenant'; *or* you can pronounce it in the evil, deformed, Forces-of-Darkness manner of Moregothic, 'lootenant'. The choice is yours.

the air through which they passed a bit neither-this-nor-that, a bit to-be-frank-with-you-vague; and they conversed amongst themselves saying, 'This is the problem with creating a world with nothing but music, very pretty but not specific enough. What's needed here are some words – give the song some shape, meaning and so on.'

And so, as they flew through the air, the Dragons spoke. And they spoke forth the sun, to burn light and heat upon the world. And they spoke forth the high air, which is blue fire and blue smoke; and they spoke the lower air, which is clear; and they spoke the mountains, and the restless oceans that chafe against the girdle of the land. And they spoke glaciers, and towering waterfalls, and deserts of sand and deserts of hard rock.

And Moregothic saw all this and, though he was surprised, yet he said, '*That's* more like it, some structure – that makes it all much clearer, yes. Words are much better at doing that than just music by itself, as it turns out.'

Now Emu in Asdar had his sleeve tugged by his Holy Ones, and they said, 'Er, Mighty One, have you seen what Moregothic is doing over in Upper Middle Earth?'

And Emu, looking round, said, 'Good *grief*. No, this won't do at all.'

And he dispatched the Spirits of the Valŭpac to Upper Middle Earth. There they found a land carved from the rugged beauty of the poetry of dragons: they found mountains like massy clouds brought down to the horizon and condensed into granite. They found wildernesses of pebbles, and deserts of red grit. They found a coastline where the sea was mad in its rage and headbutted the land over and over. And they found mighty waterfalls hurling themselves over the raw cliff in two thousand white twining lines from the black pool above, like the tentacles of a great albino sea creature.

And, seeing this, the Valŭpac spoke words of their own. For though they could not undo the speech of the Dragons yet nevertheless what they spoke chimed contrapuntally with the Dragonwords.

They spoke woods, and rolling grasslands, and the mild beasts of earth and forest. They spoke rivers that rolled as vowels down the flanks of clover-covered hills; they spoke fish that darted as consonants within those waters. They spoke birds that jewelled through the air, and butterflies which wave greeting at the world as they fly; and these birds and these butterflies are words that seem brief yet contained great wonders. And at last they spoke people to live in these beautiful places, whom they called *elves*, which, in the primary speech of creation, meant *words*.[5]

And the Valūpac departed and returned to Asdar.

The first Elves were made in the new land between the mountains Ered Loonpants and the Capital Sea. These were the Tree Elves, and they were a beautiful people, tall, with large eyes and large ears, with wide smiles and dark hair. And the first king of these Elves was called Tuoni Bleary, the King of the First Elves. And the land was called Blearyland; and in the mornings and the evenings, in memory of the original wordless song of Emu, the land was spread with cloth of mist and haze that spilled the sunlight in gold and honey, in topaz and blood. And when the sun had risen, or had gone quite behind the horizon, the land acquired the harder-edged loveliness that the Dragons had given it. And because the elven peoples thought the most beautiful views happened during the fuzzy, bleary, unfocused dawn and dusk, they did praise it in an imprecise song:

---

5 [Author's note] Compare the Latin *elevate*, from *levis* 'light', meaning to illuminate, to raise up to comprehension, to provide meaning; which is to say, 'word'.

*Look:* I *believe, very much, you know, in beauty*
*And I think it's important to recognise*
*The very important role played by, you know,*
*the beauty community. Indeed.*

And the Elves built a great city amongst the trees of Hipinonsens, north of the great forest of Taur-ea-dor-pants, and this city they called Tonjon, though the other races of Upper Middle Earth tended to call it Elftonjon, which means 'spangly top on taur-ea-dorpants'.

And King Bleary said, 'Like, you know, this is a terribly encouraging development, which represents a year-on-year increase in city-ness *in* the Blearyland area in real terms.'

And Robin 'Goodfellow' Cük, Prince of Elves said, 'Indeed, hmm, huarr, gnarr, ashahahaha,' and did make a strange high-pitched keening sort of noise.

And King Bleary promised his people a golden age. He decreed there would be a social structure that treated all elves fairly, to be called the Elf-fair State; and he decreed a National Elf Service for the treatment of sickness, and free elfucation provision.[6]

---

6  For did not King Bleary himself say his priorities were 'elfucation, elfucation, elfucation'? And did not the publishers of this volume also say 'we would like to apologise in the abjectest terms imaginable for the barrel-bottom nature of the jokes contained in this particular paragraph of the *Sellamillion*, which exceeds EU maxima for groans-per-phrase by 300%'?

And the people believed King Bleary, and there was much rejoicing throughout the whole of Blearyland.

Now Moregothic watched this latest development from his fastness in the north, which he called Cumabund, which means 'calling this place a fast-ness is, frankly, to speak ironically, since its domin-ant characteristic is on the contrary how *slow* everything is here; ice-bound wilderness, huge cyclo-pean blocks of granite, massive architecture but nothing much to do all day except plot evil plots and stare at the snow-covered landscape.' For it is some-times the case that a single short word can only be rendered into another language with a hugely lengthy paraphrase. That's just the way it is with translation, can't be helped.

And Moregothic gathered together his horde of Orks, and said unto them: 'Righto, chaps, I'm sure word has reached you of the increasing populations of Elves to the lands south of here. Now, some of you may be asking yourself, "Why did the Dark Lord himself decide to build his fastness Cumabund up here amongst the frozen wastes and black granite peaks, where nothing grows and even the crows per-ish as they fly through the air?"'

And with one voice, the five hundred thousand

Ork warriors cried, 'Oo no, my lord, the thought never crossed our minds, honestly.'

'No, no,' said Moregothic, indulgently, 'the rumours *have* reached my ears, and it's perfectly understandable. I'm not going to have anybody flayed alive for saying such a thing – I'm not a monster, after all. Well, to be exact, I *am* a monster, strictly speaking, but, well, you know what I mean. Allow me to explain.'

And the mighty horde of Orks cried, 'My lord, you're spoiling us, really you are.'

And Moregothic said, 'No, couldn't quite catch that, the legion on my left hand was slightly out of synch with the mass to my right. It came to my ears as a sort of raging confusion of noise. Something about boiling, was it?'

And the mighty horde of Orks cried, more slowly and with distinct pauses in between the words, 'My lord, you're spoiling us, really you are.'

And Moregothic said, 'Ah, yes, got it that time. Well, you're my Orks and you deserve the best. The truth is, this is a slightly rubbish location for a fast-ness – but what you need to understand is that when we came here, and the Dragons added words to Emu's music, thereby creating a much more structured and rational cosmos to live in, it was all much of a muchness. But now that Emu has sent his Valǔpac over here, they've smartened things up *no end* down south. When I was last down there it was all barren rock and hailstones, but now I hear it's pleasant woodland, parks, rivers full of fish, all manner of interesting wildlife. Anyway, anyhow, anyhew, to cut a long story short, I've decided we should invade. There's plenty of space for all, and as a special bonus we get not only to slay, but also to smash, crush, drive before us, listen to the lamentations of the severely wounded – which is to say, all your favourite hobbies.'

And the Orks did cheer; and raised their hook-ended sabres over their heads and did brandish them in the cold air.

And Sharon did say, 'Good idea, my lord.'

And so it was that a great Army of Darkness came raging out of the frozen north, and fell upon the elven populations of the more temperate south as a wolf falls upon a flock of sheep, or a hawk upon a flock of doves, although, now I come to think of it, it's rather confusing to have the same word to describe collective gatherings of sheep and birds. I mean, are there two more different sorts of creatures than, say, sheep and birds? Sorry, I don't mean to go off on one, it's just a particular bugbear of mine.[7]

So, running out of time, barely have time to tell you about the mighty battle between the Elves and the hordes of evil. Ten years of solid fighting. The forces of Darkness had it all their own way at first, but then, just when all seemed lost, you know the drill, a single heroic self-sacrifice turned the tide, I'm not sure of all the details, but that doesn't matter particularly. Anyway, finally Moregothic was overthrown and chained up, using a really big chain. And I mean *really* big.

And the mighty Elvish lords who led their different tribes in this great fight were called Tuoni Bleary, and Nodihold, and Manwëewer Lukithatime. And from their respective peoples descended the three great tribes of the Elves; the Bleary, the Nodiholdor and the Man-Wëers.

But although Moregothic was chained with the really big chains, the Elves had not captured Sharon,

---

7 Which reminds me, I meant to include the 'Bugbear' amongst the hideous progeny Moregothic created: it being, as you surely know, a gigantic half-insect, half-polar-bear hybrid, with eight albino hairy arms, mandibles instead of a mouth, big muscles, and a special iron exoskeleton that it has to keep oiled with seal-oil from fresh-caught seals. Nasty piece of work, I can tell you.

nor had they extinguished the existence of many of the Orks.[8] And they scattered into the wild wildernesses and 'wa!' wastes (so called because people often let out a cry of babyish terror on first seeing them), and lived for many generations in those places. And Nodihold did say to King Bleary, 'Should we not pursue these agents of wickedness even unto the furthest reaches of the Earth and put an end to them, for fear that they will regather, regroup, and come back to attack us another time?'

And King Bleary did say, 'What? No, clearly there is no need for the public expense of such an expedition. I mean, look: it's pretty cold up there, and *I* believe that they'll all get chills and sneeze themselves to death, or something. Intelligence reports from the Central Inelfigence Agency suggest that no further threat exists to the elven way of life.'

And Nodihold did scratch his massy elven sideburns, like unsightly growths of moss on the sides of his otherwise smooth and golden face, and did say, 'Are you sure? I mean, it seems like leaving it rather to chance. Couldn't we just send one squad of soldiers into the wilderness to make certain?'

---

8  Damn, forgot them again. This should read '. . . Orks, *and Bugbears*.'

And King Bleary said, 'I will institute a far-reaching consultative process, the Big Conelversation, to open up the process of regal governance to the Elvish people.' Which, as Nodihold knew, was King Bleary's way of saying 'no'.

And afterwards Manwëe came up to Nodihold and said, 'So? Are we going to finish what we started, or what?'

And Nodihold shook his head mournfully, and replied, 'Manwëe, we're all crazeee now.'

And Manwëe asked, 'All what?'

'Crazy,' said Nodihold, 'sorry, I had a sort of hiccough when I said that and it did something strange with the final syllable. But is it not crazy to leave our future to chance in this manner?'

And Manwëe said, 'Excuse me for a mo, I need to take a comfort break.'

And so the Elves lived in safety for a little space.

## Of The Unchaining of Moregothic

The unchaining of Moregothic is told in the Lay of Ladylay.[9] Now the Evil Lord had been chained up with these *really* big chains for ages.

And Moregothic did say to the Elves who guarded him, in the dungeons of Cumabund, 'Look, this chain is really rather uncomfortable.'

And the great Elven lord Ladylay, who was charged with guarding him, did reply, 'Hmm, well, you should have thought of that *before* you led a flesh-eating horde of Orks from the howling north to wage war upon Elfkind, shouldn't you? Eh?'

And Moregothic did reply, 'Fair point, fair point, only there's this link digging into the small of my back, very uncomfortable. Could you just slip the chain off for a mo, so I can readjust it? It'd take thirty seconds, and I promise I won't bother you any more after that.'

And Ladylay did say, 'I don't know.' And he

---

9  Also known by some authorities as 'the Lay of Crosmybigbrasbed'.

turned to his deputy Crosmybigbrasbed, and said, 'What do you reckon?'

And Crosmybigbrasbed shrugged.

'Alright,' said Ladylay. 'One minute. Only you have to promise not to try any funny business when the chain is off.'

'Funny business?' said Moregothic, as if the very thought was absurd and even offensive to him. 'Guys! Come on, guys – it's me!'

'Say "I promise".'

'I promise.'

But Ladylay was not to be fooled so easily, and he said: 'Say "I promise", followed by what it is that you promise.'

'I promise not to try any funny business when the chain is off.'

And they took off the mighty chain, and Moregothic did leg it, and Ladylay did stand holding the chain, looking like a bit of a twit really.

And Moregothic fled to the far north, and there assembled around himself his followers again. And he said to his army of Orks, 'Well it's pretty clear the one mistake *I* made was to put all my eggs in one basket, ork-wise.'

And his Orks said, 'Eggs?'

'What I need,' said Moregothic, 'is a bigger and a better army, with a fully diverse and ethnically integrated range of evil creatures.' And so he created new, bigger Orks; and also Giant Ants of Death, War-Ouliphants; and he created monstrous smooth-headed cave monsters, the Baldtrogs; and he created Goblins and hordes of terrible flesh-eating monsters. And then he said, 'That ought to do it, really.'

And word reached the Elves in the south that a mighty muster was mustering in the frozen north. And they were sore afraid. Indeed, sores were the least of the things they were afraid of. They were more afraid of being torn to blood-scattering pieces of quivering flesh, speared, devoured, and utterly killed.

## Of The Coming Of Men into Blearyland

It was during this era that a new race came to Blearyland, travelling from the east over the mountains. These were *Men*, who are mortal and proud yet had the capacity to become portly and cowed. They arrived in the elvish forest Taur-ea-dorpants, a ragged band of men and women and children. And the Elves did accost them, saying 'Hey! What are you lot doing in our forest?'

And Riturnov, who was King of these new peoples, did reply 'Is this Southlands Bec?'

And Fingorbuffet the Nibblesome, a prince of the Elves, did reply, 'No, no, you're miles off, mate – *miles* away, you should have taken the left turn at the waterfall by Ered Loonpants.'

And Riturnov did reply, 'I *knew* it, I told Harrison we was on the wrong road. Ah well, ah well, we're here now, too late to start off again today. You got anything to eat?'

At first the Elves were wary of the newcomers, who ate and drank like gannets, frankly, and who had hair growing out of every part of their bodies save only a small space around their eyes, and a second hairless patch between eyebrows and hairline, I mean yuck or *what*. For no Elf has such extensive body hair, excepting only the slight hairiness of Nodihold, and the much more extensive hirsuitery of Wiurdi the Beardy, the elf with a pelt.

Now, when Men first came to Blearyland they were fleeing an unspeakable horror in the east, and when the Elves asked Men from what it was that they fled they replied, 'Which part of "unspeakable" don't you understand? – The basic concept resides in a thing not being speakable about, alright?' After which they went '*tch*'. And the Elves were sore ashamed.

But after many months, and much drink shared, the Elves came to form an alliance with the sons of Man, and with their daughters, though not with their brothers, who were, frankly, a little standoffish.

And so King Bleary agreed a treaty with the Men of Numenorwhat? that they did take up arms together to fight the evil of Moregothic. And they told Men of Numenorwhat? lengthy epic tales of the evil of Moregothic, and of his bitter lieutenant Sharon, of his chaining up, and the unfortunate unchaining incident that happened subsequently, which was just plain unlucky, not anybody's fault actually, just one of those things.

'So the upshot, with regard to this wicked More-gothic, is that he's loose again, is he?' asked the Men. 'Just run it past us one more time, how he got free from the giant chain?'

And the Elves did hmm and ha, and did look at their shoes for a bit. Then they did say, 'But anyway – anyway – the *important* thing is that together we shall fight the forces of evil! Together we pledge our courage and our blood to defeat this terrible enemy who blights Upper Middle Earth.'

And after much ale, the Men did cry, 'Yes! Yes! Let us band together in a great alliance, and fight shoulder to shoulder against evil and tyranny!'

And the Elves did say, 'We will spill our blood gloriously, as brothers!'

And the Men did agree. 'And we shall be daunt-less,' said the Men. 'No daunting for us. We shall fight without daunt of any kind.'

'Hurrah!' cried Men and Elves together.

And when they had sobered up a bit the following day, Men returned to the elven halls and said, 'Look, *great* news about the alliance and all that, *really great* news, we're simply chuffed, we really are, it's just that, well, we were talking to these wood-hewers and they sort of, well to put it frankly, they told us that – well, let me, let me put it this way. You know this evil lord chap, and his evil lieutenant that we have pledged to fight to the last drop of blood in our veins?'

And the Elves did say, 'Yes? What about them?'

And the Men did enquire, 'Well, we were just curious, it's more, you know, curiosity than anything else. But who else is on *their* side?'

And the Elves did say, 'An army of half a million terrible Orks, Giant Ants of Death, War-Ouliphants, fifth-column ouliphants who try to infiltrate our cities and blend into the crowd to subvert our defences from within, although to be honest they're not terribly successful; Baldtrogs; Goblins; Trolls and many terrible flesh-eating monsters.'

And the Men did ask for clarification, saying, 'How many of those last lot?'

And the Elves did say, 'Hordes.'

And the Men did say 'Oh' in a small voice, and did assume a doleful countenance, which the Elves did assume was a reflection of a certain hangover, which sometimes did afflict the children of Men after the consumption of certain quantities of beer.

But the alliance was binding, and Men and Elves stood shoulder to shoulder.

## *Of The Coming Of Dwarfs into Blearyland*

It was round about this time that Elves and Men first noticed that Dwarfs had come into Blearyland. And when they taxed them with their coming, and asked from whence they came, and for why they had left that place, the Dwarfs did say, 'Been here ages bach, you just didn't notice us. Simply ages – longer'n you, I daresay, look you. Under the ground, see. Underneath, out of sight, out of mind, see.'

And the Elves did say, 'Pull the other one.'

And the Dwarfs did say, 'No, no, honestly.'

And it being impossible to prove or disprove it, one way or another, Elves and Dwarfs left it there for the time being.

And the dwarf-kingdoms of Blearyland were carved from the very living rock, but also from the dead rock, which was easier to carve actually, since it wasn't given to moaning and trembling and crying hot lava when you cut into it with a pickaxe. And the great dwarfish cities were named Khāzi, Khazhak-stān, Khizzikhizzi, Khāztofthousands and the dark dwarrow-dwelling of Khāz-by-Garinewman.

27

And the Elves did say, 'Look, I'm really sorry about this, but you just can't stay. We're just not a big enough country to accommodate whole new populations. It's not as if you're genuine asylum seekers, you're more economic migrants.'

And the Dwarfs did say, 'echo-gnomic migrants' and did laugh proudly and mightily, as if they had said something funny, and some amongst the Dwarfs did go 'Hi-ho! hi-ho!', with the second part spoken in a smaller voice as if it were an echo of the first, and this in turn did provoke the Dwarfs to further hilarity, such that they fell to the floor laughing, although they did not hurt themselves so doing, the floor not being very far for a Dwarf to fall as it happens.

And the Elves more or less gave up at this point, and left the Dwarfs to their own devices.

## Of The Coming Of Munchkins
## into Blearyland

Shortly thereafter a great army of Munchkins did arrive in Blearyland, singing mighty songs and bringing with them buildings and road design of a surprisingly advanced design, bearing in mind that the Munchkins themselves were not only just two foot tall or so but also markedly infantile and pliable. But the Elves said, 'For goodness' sake, this is just too much, I mean, I'm as much in favour of ethnic diversity as the next man, but enough's enough. Go on, you lot, away with you.' And with kicks, cuffs and general ya!-ing, they did chase the Munchkins to the borders of Blearyland and nudged them over the edge.

And the Elves did say, 'And stay out,' and did brush their hands together with alternating up-down strokes.

*Of the Great Destruction wrought by
Moregothic, and of the Attempts Made
by the Elves and Men to wreak Destruction
upon Moregothic, and of the wreakage of
Destruction upon Moregothic, which was
eventually wranged, or possibly wrekted*

So Moregothic wrought great destruction upon the lands of Blearyland. And the Elves and Men formed a mighty alliance and made war upon Moregothic in an attempt to destroy him, which attempt was ultimately successful. And Moregothic was burnt to crispy embers.

## A More Detailed Account of the Great Destruction Wrought by Moregothic, and of the Attempts Made by the Elves and Men to wreak Destruction upon Moregothic, and of the eventual Destruction of Moregothic

It has been brought to my attention that some people, I mention no names, they know who they are – that some people were, shall we say, *under*-satisfied with the previous account of the great destruction wrought by Moregothic, and the attempts made by the Elves and Men to wreak destruction upon Moregothic, and of the Destruction of Moregothic. Well, I *thought* I got straight to the pith of the matter in my previous account. But I suppose there are people for whom pith is not enough. If you want a pith-free, husk-heavy account, who am I to disagree? Your wish, my command, and so on, and so on, et cetera.

Very well then. Pay attention. I'm not going through this more than once.

Moregothic had fled even further to the north, and he built himself a new fastness which he called Winter-underland.[10] And as he constructed it, his mighty army did sing a spine-chilling song about Moregothic's new kingdom.[11]

And Moregothic planned his terrible revenge upon all of Upper Middle Earth, making sure this time to cross the 't's and dot the 'i's, the lower-case 'j's and any umlauted 'u's that needed it. 'I shall leave nothing to chance,' he told his lieutenant, Sharon. 'I have assembled an army ten times as large as my previous army, and recruited monstrous and flesh-rending shock-troops instead of a measly rabble of Orks.'

And Sharon did say, 'Good *idea*, my lord' with great enthusiasm.

And Moregothic did say, 'Isn't it, though? And I tell you what, I've had *another* good idea as well. I shall seal my invulnerability with – guess what?'

And Sharon did ponder, going, 'Hmm, hmm; oh, now, now – could it be magic?'

---

10  Because it was mostly constructed under the land. And because so far north it was always winter. To be frank, I reckon you could have worked that out for yourselves, if you'd put the effort in. But *oh* no, not you.

11  Mind you, any song can be described as spine-chilling if the spine gets chilled; and any spine will be chilled if the ambient temperature is low enough. That's common sense, that is.

'Magic, yes,' said Moregothic, and he did nod smugly. 'I shall summon the four Dragons of this world, for they are the beings in which magic is most potent. And they shall lay upon me a spell of protection so strong that not the Elves, not the Valūpac, not Emu himself could break it. I shall fashion the spell such that no chain will ever bind me again, because I don't mind telling you I didn't like that chain-up business one little bit. I shall weave the spell so cunningly that no creature shall be able to lay hand on me, or weapon, that nothing fashioned by elvish hands will be able to destroy me. I shall be invulnerable, and immortal, and shall ride to flaming victory.'

'Excellent, master!'

'Isn't it, though?'

And Sharon said, 'Could I have a similar spell made for me, master?'

'Certainly not,' said Moregothic, gruffly.

'Not even,' said Sharon, in a small voice, 'a little one?'

'Be off with you,' snapped Moregothic. 'I've no time to be worrying about underlings.'

Now the fastness of Moregothic was a huge network of tunnels and groined chambers, of corridors and deep dungeons; but one portion of it projected above the frost-hard ground, and this was a tower a thousand feet tall, seemingly slender as a white stalk of wheat against the huge backdrop of mountains, yet forty yards wide and builded of blocks of white granite interlocked more cunningly than a cun.[12] And Moregothic did climb to the very summit of this tower where the air was clear, and sword-sharp with cold. And he spoke a spell of summoning for the Dragons. And the four Dragons answered his call, and flew in the air around the tower, such that, from a distance, it seemed as though a whirlwind and snowstorm possessed the tower.

'I command you!' Moregothic cried.

But the Dragons had grown in spirit and power since their creation, and were wilful, and independent of mind; and though they hearkened to Moregothic's call yet they did hold back. For he had created them, and much of his power had passed into them; and now they were balanced between obeying him and wishing his destruction. But the voice of command compelled them.

'I command a spell from you,' cried Moregothic, throwing the words from his throat into the chill and windy air. 'I must be invulnerable to harm. There

---

12 Latin *cuneus* 'wedge'; hence 'any wedge-shaped object'. No, really.

must be no chink in my protection, no gap in the strength of magic that wraps me around.'

And the Dragon of the North sang:

> *Though only fire may kill ye*
> *Yet no flame can harm ye*
> *Yet no spark can wound ye*
> *Yet no heat can hurt ye*

And Moregothic said: 'Excellent! Yet, why do you say that fire may kill me? Can you not cast the spell such that fire has no purchase upon my body at all?' But as he asked the question he knew, in his heart, that to cast such a spell would be to quench the fire that ran in his own veins, to destroy the fire of his heart and his spirit, and that this would annihilate him. And so he contented himself with the magic that told him no flame, or spark, or heat could hurt him.

And the Dragon of the South sang:

> *Though only elf may slay ye*
> *No elf hand may touch ye*
> *No elf weapon affront ye*
> *No elf word discomfort ye*

And Moregothic made plaint, saying, 'This also is

good! Yet why should it be that even elf might slay me? Can you not cast the spell such that no creature of *any* kind has power upon me?' But as he asked the question he knew that his captivity in the dungeon of the Elves had given to them a special power over his fate that could not be undone without undoing his fate altogether, and that would annihilate him. And so he contented himself with the magic that told him no elf hand, weapon or word could hurt him.

The spell was complete. And Moregothic felt the power of the magic bind itself to his body and he cried, 'Good, good, yet must I have stronger assurance still. If I am struck with sword, arrow or spear, will that kill me?'

And the Dragons cried '*No!*'

'If I am drowned in the sea or smothered under the earth, will that kill me?'

And the Dragons cried '*No!*'

'Might man, dwarf or beast kill me?'

And the Dragons cried '*No!*'

'You say only an elf may kill me, yet no elf may kill me?'

And the Dragons cried '*So!*' And their voices were loud in the snow-thronged air.

And Moregothic said, 'That seems to tie that up.'

And he called aloud again: 'You say only fire may hurt me, yet no flame can touch me?'

And the Dragons cried '*So!*' through the mournful hissing of sleet.

And Moregothic was content, for the magic was very strong. But when such a charm is cast upon a magical being, a price is paid; and in return for this charm Moregothic surrendered part of his divinity, which passed to the Dragons. And he thought to himself, 'It matters little, for it is but a tiny splinter of my divine power, I retained the most part – and in return for this small loss I have rendered myself invulnerable. The price is worth it.' What he did not realise was that in the matter of divinity, which is infinite, a tiny portion is yet the whole, and the whole is but a splinter. But this thought did not trouble Moregothic until later.

And the Dragons departed; for they had laid their eggs in the stone of the earth, and fled away to the barrenness beyond the north where no creature save them can pass.

Now Moregothic was confident, and he led his army south, and laid waste to the west, and the fires of his army did eat up the east, and he brought flood and drouth to the south. And the Elves despaired of being able to stand against him: for his army was powerful and merciless. And the Elves cried aloud 'Woe! woe!' by which they meant to allude to their own sorrow or sadness, rather than to say 'Hey dude, slow down' or anything of that nature. And word reached them of the spells which kept Moregothic safe, which lowered morale in the elf camp even further.

The woods were burned, and the pastures defiled; elf homes and the hearths of men were trampled and destroyed, and ork and monster roamed at will. And Riturnov the King, first king of Men, was slain in a fray near a haywain, as he was lying in pain with his main troop of Men slain around him. His son Reriturnov was but a child, and the kingdom of Men was ruled by the regent, Strete.

At last the great elf-general Fimble and the War-lord of Men, Rokett, mustered the last remnant of the army of the Elves and of Men. 'Come,' he cried, 'we must drive this army of evil back whence it came.'

And the Elves mounted horses for the first time, to ride alongside the cavalry of Men; and they rode down the downs to collide with the Ork footsoldiers in the foothills; quite an impressive sight, actually, that cavalry charge. And the Army of Darkness broke in confusion.

But within three days it had remustered, and it drove hard against the Elves at the Battle of the Difficult Summe. And the Elves, counterattacking, suffered heavy casualties. For they were hampered by an overdemanding high command which ordered advancing troops to calculate the cube root of any four-digit prime in base 7 whilst walking slowly towards enemy arrow-fire.

And Fimble fled from the slaughter with only four dozen soldiers alive, the last survivors of the great army of Elves. And Rokett rode with him, with only three score of men left alive, the rump of the army of Men. They rode hard to the east, but their way was blocked by monstrous warrior-ants of prodigious size whose snippy-mandibles could sever a person in two with the merest snicky-snack, and Moregothic mocked them from his saddle on the thorax of the largest of the war ants, saying 'Elves! Don't you mess with my ants. You cut off their heads, they come *looking* for you.' And many Elves and many Men died in that place.

So the remnant of the elvish and mannish armies rode west, but ran against the edge of the land, where the ocean chafed and chewed at the strand. And so they rode north, wearing out their horses in their flight. And Moregothic's terrible army pursued by day and by night, for the taste of flesh was in their mouths, and lust-for-death was in their hearts.

As the Men and Elves rode further north, the land became more barren and cold; and snow lay in the hollows of the ground though the sun was up; and frost made mud stone. And still the Army of Darkness pursued them, so that even though their horses died the Elves were compelled to hurry further on foot. And they passed to the frozen lands where snow lay over all the ground in every season of the year like white topsoil, and sunshine reflected from the whiteness to dazzle the eyes in daytime, and starlight made the land glitter in the cloudless nights. Their breath came now as wraiths to leave their bodies like souls departing, and a great weariness was upon them. And after much suffering, which wore down the resistance of some of their number even unto death, they reached the frozen peaks of the Mountains of Byk.

The land here is broken and jagged, just as the Dragons created it at the beginning of days, with frozen waterfalls, boulders yet unsmoothed by wind or erosion, and harsh spires of ice reaching up to the sky in defiance. And Fimble said, 'We have come to the most terrible place in Upper Middle Earth. Here we shall make a stand. For we cannot flee forever.'

And Rokett spoke, saying, 'No, I suppose not.'

Here the last of the warrior elves and the last of the warrior men climbed the lower peaks of Mount Ezumasrevenge, and prepared to make their last stand, side by side. 'Perhaps,' said Rokett, 'we may yet slay Moregothic.' But they remembered the words of the Dragons' Spell, and knew that their swords and arrows were useless against him. 'At least,' said Fimble, 'we shall die gloriously.' And the other Elves said, 'Er, great, yeah, that's certainly a consolation,' and they added sotto voce 'as we contemplate our imminent and bloody deaths.'

Moregothic arrayed his horde around the base of Mount Ezumasrevenge, cutting off all possible escape, and then he made camp for three days and three nights. And as the last dozen elven warriors and the last score of Men shivered on their crag, the army of Moregothic feasted and danced beside giant fires; and the sound of singing, and the smell of cooked food wafted through the night.

The sun rose on the last day; and elf and man prepared themselves each of them to fight and each of them to die, for there was no hope. And at Moregothic's order, Orks and Baldtrogs swarmed up the lower slopes. Battle was short, sharp and shocking; many Orks and several Baldtrogs fell slain, but also slain were six of the twelve Elves and half the small force of Men.

And Moregothic pressed the attack with his monsters, ants, wargs, trolls and other nasties; and though they fought bravely the last warriors could not withstand, and withdrew further up the mountain.

And Moregothic called after them, 'Fools! Whither do you fly? Can you take wing like the birds of the air and soar to safety?' And he laughed, saying, 'You are already dead.'

And he marched himself into battle, for he had no fear of elf or man, protected as he was by the most powerful spell the new world had ever seen.

Seeing him approach, Fimble ran forward, carving a path through the bodies of furious Orks with his sword and his right arm. And Fimble struck at Moregothic with his sword, but the Dark Lord was proof against the weapon and it shattered like glass blade striking stone. Fimble's heart despaired at this, for he knew that the Dragon magic protected Moregothic against any assault he might make. And yet even in his despair did his courage flare up; for despair can feed rage as straw a fire, to burn bright though briefly.

And, weaponless, Fimble leapt upon the armour of

Moregothic, and struggled upwards like a mountaineer, and placed his hands around Moregothic's neck to throttle him. But no elf hand might hurt the Dark Lord, and where his hands touched Moregothic's flesh his hands burned within like acid, and dissolved away to reeking smoke. And Fimble lifted away the stumps of his arms in agony.

Moregothic laughed to see this. 'And is this the greatest warrior the Elves can send against me?' he mocked. 'A handless cripple and his band of stragglers? Though it be said only Elves might slay me, yet is it also decreed in Dragon magic that no elf hand might hurt me, no elf weapon assail me.'

And Fimble, howling in rage, threw himself forward with his last strength; and he bit with his mouth at the Dark Lord's very face, and bit again, and bit a third time. Handless as he was, armed with no weapon and speaking no word, yet Fimble struck at Moregothic.

And the Dark Lord cried in surprise and pain, and smote at Fimble with his black-bladed sword; but Fimble clung on, even as the blade cut his flesh. And Moregothic staggered in pain, and his foot stumbled on the edge of the crag, and so he fell.

His fall was mighty, and he fell hard upon the broken ground, where the stalagmite spires of ice rose up needle-sharp. And one mighty blade of ice pierced Moregothic's breast as he fell upon it and it thrust through. And he lay in pain on the frozen ground, impaled upon this terrible shaft.

And at this moment Moregothic knew that the Dragons had deceived him. For the ice pierced his chest, and its terrible cold burned his heart, and chill seared his flesh; and so he died. And with his death a great terror fell upon his soldiers; and they fled wailing and crying to the furthest reaches of the frozen wastes; and many fell into crevasses, or starved amongst the forbidding peaks. And Sharon found his way to Moregothic's Winter-underland, and there he hid himself in the deepest dungeons and nursed the terror in his heart at the death of his master and his maker.

And the last six Elves gathered the body of Fimble from the dead face of Moregothic, and burnt him in honour on a warrior's pyre. And the last of the Men took the body of Moregothic and cut it to pieces with their swords; for, being dead, he was beyond harm, and so the spell was broken and their swords could cut. And Elves and Men took a brand from Fimble's funeral pyre, and set fire to a bonfire on which they burnt the remains of Moregothic to cinder and ash; for, being dead, he was beyond harm, and so the flames could now consume him. And so Moregothic was overthrown.

And the last Elves made their way back to the warm south, and rejoined their women and their children; and over many years they rebuilt their nation. And the Men returned as heroes, and were cheered in the streets. Although after a solid ten months of them relating their war stories, the general population did get a bit bored with hearing them over and over, and tended to adopt slightly fixed, pixilated expressions when they heard the opening sentences of one of the stories, and put their minds elsewhere.

# Part 2
# The Sellamillion:
# The History of the Sellāmi

## The Theft of the Giant Sellāmi

Now in Asdar did Emu reside, and he was happy, mostly, although the afternoons did sometimes seem perhaps a trifle on the long side, and time sometimes hung a *little* heavy on his hands. But by and large it was pleasant enough, and Emu did occasionally cast a glimpse over the waters to Upper Middle Earth, and have a long look, and then turn back to Asdar. And only once did he travel to Upper Middle Earth, and that for a brief time as it can be told below; and never again did he come to that land.

In Upper Middle Earth the days were marked by the sun rising and setting, and in the night-time the stars wheeled around the hub star in the northern sky. But the sun and the stars are material things, and they cast no light in Asdar, which is no material realm. Instead Emu had constructed a gigantic pole of gold, and at the top he placed a giant Sellāmi, crafted by his own hands. This strange and beautiful thing Emu imbued with great magical power, by processing the bounty of Asdar into a single mysterious artefact, something like a jewel: long, and slender, with gorgeous facets of pinky-red and dazzling white. And in this object Emu captured the light of illumination, and a certain flavour of brilliance; and he fixed it atop the tall pole. And it cast a great light over Asdar, and the inhabitants of that blessed realm said 'Ooh, isn't that pretty, that's *much* better, being able to *see* and everything, no more banging inadvertently into things and not knowing who you were talking to and so on, and indeed carrying on talking, thinking you were talking to somebody even though they'd actually moved away.'

And for a long age the beings in Asdar were content under the light of the Sellāmi.

But in Upper Middle Earth, the evil Sharon roused himself in the lightless dungeons of Winterunderland. And with the destruction of his Master Moregothic his power had diminished greatly. But though weak in evil he was still cunning; and he said to himself, 'If I steal the Sellāmi of Emu, then its potency will restore me.' And Sharon then said to his highest-ranking Orks 'I shall create a monster to terrify the world!'

And his Orks said, 'Yes! yes, my lord, bring terror to the world with your evil creation.'

'A dog,' I think, said Sharon, thoughtful.

To which his Orks replied, 'Um, OK, a dog, alright, I suppose so.'

'I mean,' said Sharon, hurriedly, 'a really *big* dog. No laptop pooch. A man-in-a-suit size dog. *Really* big teeth. A scary dog.'

'Scary, yes,' said his Orks, warming to the notion. And they added, 'Yes, why not. A dog – a hound, yes.'

And so Sharon created a monstrous dog; a huge beast with eyes like glowing coals and a hideous slaver. And he said to his Orks, 'Actually I was thinking of giving him something truly terrifying – put down that tankard of blood-wine, Yrkh. I don't want you to spill it on my leather carpet in terror when I say this – that's right – I was thinking of giving my monstrous dog—'

'Yes, my lord?'

'What, my lord?'

'—giving it – luminous fur!' And the evil Lord Sharon looked about his followers with eager eyes. 'What do you think, eh? Eh? *Pret*-ty *terr*-if-fying I should say. Don't you think? Don't you think that's the most terrifying thing you ever heard of? Eh? What? Eh?'

And the Orks looked frankly nonplussed, giving one another eyebrow-shrugging looks in what they hoped was a surreptitious manner, said, 'Er, very good my lord.'

'*Isn't* it?' said Sharon, earnestly. 'Isn't it, though? Puts the willies up *me*, I don't mind telling you, just thinking about it. The fur is *luminous* you see.'

'Right,' said Yrkh. 'Yes. I, er, see.'

'Yes, my Lord,' said another Ork, whose name has not been recorded by history. 'Willies, yes.'

'Ooo,' said Sharon, shuddering. 'Just the *thought* of it. It's like regular fur, only . . . it *glows in the dusk*! Ugh!'

And the teeth of this monstrous hound were long and pointy, but worse than their pointyness was their colour, a sort of yellowy-cream colour with little brown flecks. Most horrible was the pong that emanated from them. And the name of this hound was The Hound of the Bark-Evil, this being the most intimidating name Sharon could think of. 'Because,' he said, 'he is a hound of darkness and his very bark will be a bark of evil.'

'Excellent idea,' said the Orks, looking over their shoulders as if somebody they absolutely had to talk to right now had just walked into the room, even though no such person had in fact come in. 'Terribly scary. No, really.'

And Sharon sensed that his underlings were not as

scared by the whole luminous dog thing as he was, and said in a brisk tone, 'Yes, well, there we go, hideous hound. But I've also, actually, been thinking – maybe we need a *second* hideous creature to aid our evil schemes. I mean, in addition to the dog.'

And he mustered his army of Orks, and corralled the warrior ants together in the lowest of the low dungeons. And with monstrous science, and with the eye-gore harvested from hideously tortured victims, and a mutant assistant called Igor, he produced a hideous monstrosity, a vast warrior ant, thirty feet high, with huge protuberant compound eyes and alarmingly snickersnack mouthparts. And this creature Sharon called Ughganggooligooligooligooli-wojda-ant, or Ughgooglyant for short.

And Sharon led his army to the coast, and built a mighty port, which he called 'Starboard' just to be awkward. And here he ordered that, for miles around, the trees be felled, and the timber be cutted; and his Orks did ask, 'You mean, oh Dark Lord, the trees should be *fallen*, and the timber *cut*?' 'Yes,' said Sharon. 'That.'

And the Orks built a great fleet of boats, shaped like ducks, with tall carved prows shaped like duck-heads, and broad bases like ducks' undersides, and a little sticky-outy platform at the back. And these ships were dedicated to Wickedness; and Sharon called these ships Duck-W for that reason. W for Wicked, you see? And he sailed through the cold waters of the Capital C[13], and through the swell where the sea was green as turf and the hills of water shifted sluggishly, raising the ships up and dropping them down. And Emu, seeing this fleet approach the shores of Asdar, sent a great storm to sink the fleet; but the Duck-Ws were built robustly, and though the waters turned white, and waves thrashed and roiled, and the sea went all epileptic, yet still did they not sink.

'How are they doing that?' said Emu. 'I deliberately put a bleeding great ocean between Upper Middle Earth and Asdar to prevent things like this. How are they managing to avoid drowning?'

'They have built,' said the Valūpac in subdued voices, 'craft from wood, O Creator.'

And Emu said, 'You mean to tell me that that wood stuff *floats*? Well split my liver with a brass harpoon, I had *no* idea.'

And the Valūpac said, somewhat sheepishly, 'Um, didn't we, er, tell you about the floatiness when we created the trees, oh Lord? I thought we did. I mean,

---

13  Capital *Sea*. Sorry.

we certainly meant to tell you. Perhaps it got crowded out by all the other things we had to tell you.'

And Emu did look very severely at them. And he did mutter to himself crossly, 'Bloody great things, don't *look* like they should float, honestly, incompetence, it really is.'

And so it was that Sharon led an army of Orks, together with a giant luminous dog and a monstrous giant ant, into the fabled paradise of Asdar. And battle was joined.

The Valūpac did flash through the sky like lightning, and they felled Orks with great strokes of fire from the clouds; but Sharon mounted upon the neck of his gigantic ant, or 'gigantiant' for short.[14] And he galloped away over the hills of Asdar, with the great hound barking at its heels. Or, now that I come to think of it, perhaps not 'heels'. I think I'm in the right when I say that ants don't actually have, you know, *heels*; their legs probably go straight down to, I don't know, hooves, is it? But you know what I mean; the monstrous ant – well, I was going to say 'scuttling', since I suppose that's what ants do; but let's be honest, 'scuttling' just isn't a big enough word to describe the great lolloping strides of its twenty-foot legs.

---

14 Or 'gigant' for even shorter.

And on the beach the Valūpac put terror in the hearts of the army of Orks, and destroyed their ships utterly, and chased them into the sea. But Sharon was not amongst the slain.

And soon Sharon and his gigant and his dog arrived in that part of Asdar called Isle of Langahans, where the great pole, not a lamp-post, honestly, more just a pole that happened to have a light-emitting object at the top of it, was situated.

And the hideous hound of Sharon did sniff monstrously at the base of this great pole, and then, again monstrously, did relieve itself by raising one of its monstrous legs. And the Valūpac went, 'Urh, that's *foul*.'

At which Sharon did laugh aloud, for he rejoiced in the epithet 'foul'.

And Ughgooglyant did cut at the base of this pole with his terrible chitinous mouthparts, and did sever it through, such that it fell over with a mighty crash. And Sharon did wrap the fallen Sellāmi in grease-proof paper and tuck it inside his Evil Jacket. And, casting through his mind for the right thing to say at such a momentous moment, he called aloud, 'Aha! Ahahahah!'

And the Hound of the Bark-Evil did bark in

an evil way, and did snap at anybody who came close.

And Emu said, 'This is plain rubbing me up the wrong way and no mistake.' And he did lay a trail of gigantic luminous sausages over the pastures of Asdar in a sort of meaty dotted line. And the hideous hound of Sharon gobbled up the sausages one after the other, and was thereby led away from his Master, and over a hill, where Emu was waiting with a frying-pan of monstrous size. And he did smite the great dog on the head with this pan, and lay him low.

'Sharon,' he called, 'your Orks have been pushed into the sea by my Valūpac, and your dog has been felled!'

'Fallen,' Sharon called back. 'And I don't care.'

'Give way!' called Emu. 'Your blasphemous assault upon my paradise has been rebuffed. Your evil has broken over the rock of Asdar and fallen away like the fleeting ocean wave.'

But the laughter of Sharon was raucous and jibeish. 'The Sellāmi is mine,' he called. 'I shall carry it back to the fastness of the Winter-underland, where a great cleaver is waiting to cut it into many slivers – and with these fragments I shall grow strong. The power of your magic will sustain me for eons.'

'There's no escape,' called Emu. 'You are surrounded. Your ships have been destroyed, your army vanquished. Surrender!'

And Sharon called back, 'You'll never take me alive, Creator!'

'Don't be a fool, Sharon,' called Emu.

And Sharon fired out half a dozen bolts of foul magic, and Emu and the Valūpac ducked their heads behind the hills of Asdar. And then Sharon spoke to his ant, saying, 'I hereby promote you to queen.'

And Ughgooglyant sprouted great grey-silver wings, and launched into the air, carrying Sharon away from Asdar, and back over the wide waters of the Capital S[15], to Upper Middle Earth.

The blessed beings in Asdar did watch him fly off with heavy hearts; and, since he was taking the Sellāmi with him, darkness fell over the land of Westersupanesse. And Emu, Creator of all things, Supreme Being, did say: 'Oh.' And then did add: 'botheration.'

The great ant Ughgooglyant landed in the mountains of Byk, in Upper Middle Earth, and Sharon did

---

15  Sorry. This should be C, obviously.

rejoice. 'Yea, now I possess the sacred Sellāmi, and it shall make me strong.'

As for Ughgooglyant, he, or perhaps I should say she as it turns out, tucked her wings back against her carapace and crawled into a deep cave in the mountainside, where he, she, it, whatever, laid many eggs, spawning hideous progeny that, although much smaller than their terrible parent, yet troubled the lives of Men and Elves for eons to come, spoiling their picnics, crawling in lines round the edges of their kitchens, and so on.

Emu was not pleased by this development. But, since the land of Asdar was cast into darkness by the loss of the Sellāmi, his Valūpac could not see the expression on his face, and decided to be hopeful about things.

'Well,' said Emu. 'First, I am *seriously* considering going over to Upper Middle Earth to have a word with that Sharon chap.' And the Valūpac were astonished, for Emu had never before travelled to Upper Middle Earth, and the rumour had gone round that he didn't like to travel actually.

'But most pressing on my to-do list,' said Emu, 'I'm going to reroute this ocean so that it doesn't lead directly to Asdar for any invading army that feels like floating here on those tree things that you made in Upper Middle Earth – and they looked so massive and heavy, too. Never crossed my *mind* that they'd be able to float in water.'

The Valūpac coughed, and mumbled something in reply here that was neither particularly audible nor supposed to be.

And Rhengo spoke up, saying, 'If you reroute the ocean such that it no longer leads here, where *will* it lead?'

'Oh,' said Emu, airily. 'I'll link it through an inter-dimensional gateway, and it'll turn up somewhere or other.'

## Of The Great Battle of Taur-en-Ferno and the Disembodifying of Sharon

For many generations, Elf and Man had lived in peace in Upper Middle Earth. But now Sharon the Evil rose from the ashes of Moregothic's fall. With the great power of the Sellāmi of Emu, he was restored in evil; and he was able to use the immense power of the artefact to create for himself an army of wicked creatures: Baldtrogs, Giants, Scalyticks, I-Spiders with Maia-lidlaiders, Lurkers, Shirkers, Berks, Urks, Orks and Southwogs. And he led this army out from the frozen north to attack the south, and so avenge the death of Moregothic in the blood of Men and Elves.

This great force cut a swathe of destruction up through Illbhavior, and then cut a second swathe back down through Lothlomondwisky. Then they cut half a swathe, well a little over half if I'm being honest, let's say three-fifths, although it wasn't precisely that fraction, a shade under, alright if you want the exact number twenty-nine fiftieths of a swathe of destruction up into Blearyland. And they mustered at Taur-en-Ferno.

And Lord Sharon triumphed, ordering his men to sing 'We Are The Evil Champions' in mockery of Creator Emu's well-known predilection for sing-songs and all that. But, try as he might, he could not coordinate the voices of half a million evil creatures, such that the song which should have gone

*We Are The Evil Champions, My Friend*
*And We'll Try our Hardest to Offend*

instead sounded like a non-specific *waah-wooh* ocean of roaring that lurched upwards two tones and a semitone for 'hardest' but otherwise bore no relation to any tune known to man or elf. 'Alright, alright,' Lord Sharon ordered his horde, 'that's enough singing, blimey, what a racket.' And there was silence for a little space, with a little muttering, but then you'd expect a bit of muttering with a horde of half a million.

And against this fearful foe was assembled the great Army of Light. I mean light in the sense of *illumination* of course, sunlight and goodness and such, not light as in 'not heavy'. Some of these soldiers of the Light were very heavy indeed, let me assure you. I don't, by the way, mean 'fat', when I say that. I was going for more a sort of spiritual gravitas, combined with some big swords and, you know, shields and things.

Anyway, not to go off the point.

Emu, Lord of Light, Creator of the Cosmos, arrived at Taur-en-Ferno three hours late, saying, 'Sorry, sorry, something popped up at the last minute, what's going on here then?'

Now the Valūpac, Lords of Light, Lieutenants of Emu, were Gion, Poll, Gorge and Thingo; and they had assembled together a great army of the Good: Elves, Men, Dwarfs and some others whose names and addresses have been withheld at their own request. And this army occupied the higher ground at Taur-en-Ferno, arrayed in great ranks of gleaming golden armour and silver spears. And their helms shone in the light, and the sunlight glistened off their helmets, which as I'm sure I don't need to tell you are different things to helms, common mistake that, people always getting them confused. And their greaves were bronze. On their . . . um, legs, I think it is, that's where greaves go. Shins, I think. Or perhaps they're more sort of a codpiece. Anyway, anyway, that's not the important thing: the important thing is that their armour was all very neat and lovely, shiny in the sunshine, and there was *lots* and *lots* of it, armour, I mean, because there were just *loads* of soldiers – thousands and thousands, all properly arranged in neat ranks. As opposed to Sharon's army of evil beings, which was more like a rabble, people milling around, talking amongst themselves whilst their officers addressed them, and otherwise being disorderly. Really, behaving shockingly. Speaking with their mouths full. Scratching themselves. I'm sure you get the picture.

And Lord Poll, the Valūpac, knelt before Emu, Creator of the Cosmos, and said, 'Sire, we were awaiting your coming to lead our mighty army against the forces of Darkness, here arrayed before us, that ye may smite them utterly from Upper Middle Earth.'

And Emu did say, 'Right, lead the mighty army, I see. Well, that's all very fine and dandy and, you know, excellent, but the thing is I'm more involved in the *music* line of things. Less army ordering-about, and more, you know, singing and such.'

And Lord Poll said, 'But sire, your loyal men await your omnipotence to vanquish evil utterly and trample it before you.'

And Emu said, 'I *could* do that, yes, could do that, of course. But, the thing is, well, to put it at its simplest, I'm a lover, not a fighter. And, besides,

you're doing such a good job here that I think I'll just
– just –' And mighty Emu did smile weakly, and
look over his own ineffable shoulder at the lands of
Westersupanesse from whence he had come as if he
had just remembered something he had left there
that he really needed to pop back for, right this
minute.

And Lord Poll said, 'But Lord, the army assembled by Evil Sharon is great, and mighty in its
malignancy, and moreover has something of a hooli-
gan look about it, like it's all about to kick off.'

And Emu said, 'Tell you what, tell you what, I'll
have a quick – you know, do a quick – parley
thingumy, with Sharon. OK?'

And Emu, Master of Creation, did fly through the air
over the host, taking the form of a hippogriff, and did
reveal himself as Lord of Light on a patch of turf
where Sharon happened to be standing.

And Sharon mocked the Lord of All. 'Ha!' he
called, 'look who it isn't.' And his crack-o-doom
troops, the personal bodyguard of fang-toothed
Wargs, echoed, 'Har-har-har!', which as you know
I'm sure is the more withering and dismissive form
of the more conventional 'ha-ha-ha'. And Sharon
mocked and jibed, saying 'Well *upon* my soul if it

isn't the Lord of Creation. How *nice* of you to pop by. How *well* you're looking. Did you lose weight?' and other words of a similarly insincere and ironical nature.

And the fang-toothed Wargs said, 'Har-har, good one, my Lord.'

And Emu, Prince of Creation, did say, 'I'm warning you, your army is going to get a *pret*-ty *blood*-y nose if you insist on, you know, all the fighting and such.'

And Sharon said, 'You're warning me, are you? Some nerve, that is. We shall micturate from an elevated position upon your boys, that's what we'll do.' And he laughed at his own circumlocutionary mode of speaking, whereby a vulgar slang expression is rephrased in a more pompous and elevated idiom for comic effect. For such things amused him, and he liked to say *extracting the michael* and *go forth and multiply* and *Robert is your mother's brother* and things along those lines.

And Emu said, 'Well, all I'm saying is, wouldn't it be better for your lot to disband, not that I'm reading the riot act or anything.'

And Sharon said, 'You don't frighten me.'

And Emu said, 'Oh, *don't* I.'

And Sharon said, 'No.'

And Emu said, 'Oh, *don't* I.' And he waved his hand, and Sharon lost all corporeal form, and his armour clattered to the turf in a great pile.

And Sharon said, 'Oi!' in surprise and alarm.

And Emu, looking round about with an innocent expression said, 'Sorry, what?'

And Sharon said, 'You pack that in, you've magicked away my corporeality, you cheater. Just you undo that spell, undo it *right now*, oo, I feel most queer, lacking all material bodily existence all of a sudden.'

And Emu said, 'Who, me?' with wide eyes.

And Sharon said, 'Don't act all innocent with me, Buster.'

And there was a great sucking in of breath by the fang-toothed Wargs, for Sharon in his pride had dared so daringly as to call the creator of all things Buster.

And Emu said, 'I don't know what you're talking about.'

And Sharon said, 'Yeah, right, like anybody else around here is liable to deprive a person of their corporeal form with a wave of their finger. Just give me back my body, and then we can get on with the, you know, fighting and warring and such.'

And Emu said, 'What's it got to do with me?'

And Sharon said, 'Now, come along, play fair. You are supposed to be the fair one, after all.'

And Emu said, 'Oh, give you back bodily form, is it?'

And Sharon said, 'If you don't mind.' And he spoke with a certain primness.

And Emu said, 'Well.'

And he waved his other hand, and Sharon resumed bodily form, but not the form he had had before. For where before he had been a towering shape of blackness, with mighty limbs and mightier thews, assuming thews come in the plural, as I think they do, not *entirely* sure what thews are, but pretty sure that Sharon's previous form had included them and that they were mighty – anyway.

— now he was a gigantic eyeball. He lay now upon the sward, three feet across, globular, and filled with vitreous humour. And he was squashy, lacking any internal skeleton or form; and bits of grass and grit did adhere to his moist, adhesive outer layer, causing him thereby some considerable discomfort, I don't mind telling you. Yet being one of the Valūpac, albeit a fallen one, Sharon could still speak. And he said, 'Stop mucking about, this is no good, I've not even got limbs.'

And Emu said, 'Corporeal form, didn't you say?'

And Sharon said, 'How am I supposed to pick up me sword? Couldn't you at least give me a tentacle or something? A tentacle, that is, with a, you know, opposable thumb, so that I can wield a sword? Or something?'

And Emu said, 'Is that the time? Look, I'd love to chat, I really would, but I have to fly.'

And Sharon said, 'What, not even an eyelid? Come on, one single eyelid, that can't be too much to ask. I'll get retinal burn-out without it.'

And Emu, Lord of Creation, transformed ineffably into a gigantic moth, and flew off, becoming a little distracted by a nearby campfire but soon sorting himself out and returning to Westersupanesse, never again to travel to the lands of Upper Middle Earth.

And Sharon's personal bodyguard picked up the Lord of Darkness, and wrapped him in the softest blanket they could find, although it wasn't especially soft, the quartermasters of Evil having earlier received strict instructions not to make their blankets too easy on the skin for fear of mollycoddling the troops of Darkness. And they laid him in a tent, where he complained bitterly about the twigs stuck round the back of his eyeball.

And the battle of Taur-en-Ferno was joined, and great was the slaying, the slayage, the slay-total, slayen, um, great was the number of the slain, and fires burnt the massive trees of the forest, causing the squirrels and birds to be trapped in the upper branches, until brave fire-squirrels fought their way up in little red outfits and rescued as many of the trapped as they could.

And after the battle was finished the Army of Darkness was in retreat over the lands of South Blearyland, although the Army of Light was also pretty pooped, and had been reduced to one-twelfth of its original size, what with casualties and so on.

And Sharon retreated to the grimly named land of Moider![16] And he ordered his Warg bodyguard to carry him to the very top of the tall tower of Cirith Connoli, where they positioned him under a sort of makeshift umbrella. And Sharon was even sourer in mood than before, and plotted a terrible revenge upon the world.

---

16  [*Author's note*] It is unclear whether this exclamation mark represents a glottal stop, or the mortal remains of an unfortunate parchment weevil who got under the elbow of one of the scribes. Gruf the Dwarf was the first of the free peoples to see this land with his own eyes; he returned in dismay, calling aloud 'It's Moider!, I tell ya!'

## Of the New Way of King Bleary and the Effect This Had Upon the Elves of Upper Middle Earth

King Bleary the Elf called a great moot, or meet, one of the two, I'm not sure, could have been either one to tell you the truth, I had a sort of bunged-up condition afflicting my orifices when this story was related to me and to my wax-packed ears the two words sound exactly alike. But the important thing is that they met at the moot.

Or mot at the meet.

I fear I'm straying from the point.

'Elves,' said King Bleary, 'first of all, well done on defeating evil. But. Look: we need to improve our casualty reduction target-achievement-rates. And we need to reprioritise our strategic realignments. I've decided to take *personal* charge of the "Ultimate Evil: Just Say No" campaign.'

And, at his side, Robin 'Goodfellow' Cük, Prince of Elves said, 'Wearhllll *eek*! hmm grmm mnmm personcharsayno,' and concluded with a strange high-pitched whinnying.

And the King roused the moot with a great speech. 'We need a better tomorrow for Elves. And a better tomorrow after that tomorrow, and a better tomorrow after that tomorrow the day after tomorrow. This is not the end. It is not the beginning of the end. It is not the end of the beginning, nor the end of the end, nor the middle ending of the beginning's end – no! We have not reached. The end of our endeavour, nor. The ending of the endeavour's proper end. Indeed, it is quite hard to pinpoint exactly where we are on the line between beginning and end, except to say that we *are* on that line, and this I say to you without fear or favour. Let us therefore. Brace ourselves to do our duty. And move into the broad sunlit elflands of a brighter tomorrow, a cleaner, healthier, fairer, better, elfier tomorrow. Yet, if we work together. We can put behind us the hindmost, move beyond the hindsight, hinder the hinds. What is our aim? Victory, victory at all costs, victory never mind the price, costless victory, pricelessness, however victorious the victory may be.'

And the Elves were most impressed by this, and cheered their king loudly. And then the King said:

'After extensive negotiations with Lord Sharon I am pleased to say that we, the Elven people, are able now to extend the hand of friendship to the Orkadian peoples. With the best qualities of Lord Sharon's belief-system matched with the core values of our own, the future is bright. Thank you, Emu bless you, and Emu bless Elflandia!'

Now Nodihold did say, 'Er, what was that last bit, sire?'

'Emu bless Elflandia.'

'No, sire, the bit before the Emu bless bit?'

And King Bleary smiled. 'For too long,' he said, 'our land has been riven by the tired old ideologies of "good" and "evil". It is time for us to wake up to the truth of the modern world, that so-called "goodness" does not work – however noble its aims it ignores the reality of human nature, it cannot generate wealth or provide the social cohesion necessary for a modern elvish state. These tired and exploded dreams have dogged us for too long! I say to you, the road to the future is neither "good" nor "evil", but a third way, a Bleary new ideology. Lord Sharon and I have had a number of very fruitful and productive meetings on this matter. I'm pleased to report that he is the sort of Being of Evil I can do business with.'

'But – sire,' said the Elves assembled there, 'have we not dedicated ourselves to fighting Sharon and all that he stands for?'

'Which,' said Bleary, 'is *exactly* the point I am making. It's so last-generation, this knee-jerk denigration of Sharon's achievements. True, I have not always been in agreement with his personal style. But it is foolish to deny his many achievements, in slimming down the Upper Middle Earth economy—'

'—killing and laying waste—' cried Nodihold.

'—which are,' said Bleary, speaking more loudly and fixing his face in a more resolute expression as if to say *hecklers will not intimidate me, I speak out fearlessly*, 'which are both very effective ways in slimming down an economy, or indeed a country, cutting out the surplus fat and making Upper Middle Earth competitive on the global and interdimensional stages. My Blearyist way forward combines Sharonite vigour and energy with the best of the traditional "goodness" which has always been a proud part of elven politics.'

And the Elves were confused, and did say, 'Um, I don't know, sounds plausible I suppose . . .' whilst others did say, 'It's a betrayal of all that elfishness means', and so the debate continued, and King Bleary remained king for a little space.

But eventually the Elves realised that their king was a shyster of shocking depravity, and cast him from the throne, and exiled him from elflands forever. And he was compelled to go seek succour with Lord Sharon; and the former Prince Robin Goodfellow was renamed Robin Badchap, and sent away with his master, though he complained the whole time that he had been misunderstood, and that everything he said had been to contradict what Bleary had argued, yet could nobody understand his complaint, any more than they had been able to understand his original comments, and so his doom was sealed. And the Elves raised up a new king, called Gondor 'the Brownie'.

# *Of the Rage of Sharon*

Now did Sharon concentrate and magnify his rage and despite.[17] And his vassals grew more afraid of him than before, since although he was only a gigantic eyeball nevertheless he was powerful, his will was strong, and few could stand beneath his stare without themselves blinking or looking away. And his Ork captains called him 'Stare-Master' and were themselves often starestuck in his presence.

But Sharon did complain mightily, saying 'It's *extremely* uncomfortable, I don't mind telling you, being a giant eye with no eyelid. I've got this permanent spot of blankness *right in the middle* of my field of vision. I didn't realise until this moment just how constricted the focusing power of the eye is – only a small percentage of the retina focuses a sharp image; most of the rods and cones relate movement, shade and colour in rather vague terms. And without eyelids the cells in that central portion of my

---

17   This sentence is either incomplete, or else it isn't. On balance I think I'll plump for the latter.

retina are frankly overstimulated, and are burning out.'

And Lord Sharon's retinal fatigue did make him vastly grouchy. And accordingly he planned a huge war against Elves and Men to take his mind off it, as far as that was possible.

And though he possessed mastery over his followers, yet he possessed none of the motor anatomy or eyeball-musculature that moves the eyes in other creatures; and so to look upon something new he perforce must order one of his underlings to pick him up and physically relocate him.

At the beginning this process was uncertain, and Orks would lift his great spherical bulk with their faces averted, and expressions indicative of considerable distaste, for the skin of Sharon was slimy and unpleasantly pliant, and he did not smell good.

And on one occasion, Sharon, at the top of his tall tower in Moider!, ordered members of his personal Orkish bodyguard to re-orient him by lifting him and swivelling him through twenty degrees the better to view happenings on the Plains of Polcadot many leagues distant and far below his vantage point. But the Orks charged with this great deed did fumble, and jabbing Sharon in the tender part of the eyeball with an armoured knuckle, did make him call out 'Oi, watch it, clumsy', which inspired them with such terror that they dropped the great eyeball of Sharon.

And the eyeball of evil did fall from its special podium, and roll across the tower's topmost platform. And Sharon did call out 'He-e-ey! O-o-oh!'

And as the Orks scrambled to retrieve the eyeball they did collide with one another in their haste and terror, and one of them was in such fear that he ran hard into the side of the podium, breaking his nose.

And Sharon's eyeball rolled perilously close to the top of the spiral staircase, which staircase ran the whole length of the height and depth of the tall tower. And Sharon wavered on the top step. 'Quickly,' he called, 'catch me – use your foot if you have to – before I aaaaaiiiii!' And it was too late.

And Sharon did bump down the many stone steps of the spiral staircase, saying 'Ow! Ow! Ow!' all the way down. And at the bottom he did bounce surprisingly high, saying as he travelled through the air 'Oh noo-oo-*ooo*'. And an Ork soldier at the bottom made a flying leap to try and grab the Dark Lord in the air, but only succeeded in knocking him with an outstretched hand, such that he flew in a great arc through the main gate of the Tower of Cirith Connoli, and rolled away down the parched grassy bank outside. And the Lord of all Darkness finally came to rest in a ditch, pupil-downwards, and as his quivering Orks retrieved him from this undignified position he did say, in a worryingly calm-sounding voice, 'I am *far* from happy about this, I can tell you all *that* right now.'

And after Lord Sharon had been carried back up all the steps and reinstalled on his special podium, underneath the umbrella, he did order a severe punishment of the Orks who had handled him so clumsily.

And after this came Bleary the fallen elf to Cirith Connoli, abashed and cast out by his own people, and Robin Badfellow with him. And Bleary did say to Sharon. 'Look, I know that politics, ruling people, involves some tough choices. Some hard choices. Toughness and hardness. And I say, you know, *I'm* the man to make those tough choices and hard choices. There are those who say, Tuoni, *be* soft and weak, but I say, I'm sorry, that's just not the sort of elf I am. So I say *to* you, Sharon, look: you're a leader. On the world stage. And I'm a leader. On the world stage. You're a person who spans the generations, and who has been a source of inspiration, of one sort or another, to practically everyone. And so am I. So, *let* us put our differences behind us, and. Agree an alliance between our two great peoples.'

And Sharon did reply, 'My spies tell me you've been ignominiously kicked out of Elfland as a traitor.'

'Look,' said Bleary, 'a lot of things have been said by a lot of people. But let. Me just say this. We'll respond to those charges. At the proper time. And not before. We'll respond *after* the official enquiry has concluded its work. It would be quite wrong for me to prejudge the outcome of that enquiry.'

'You come to me as a worm crawls on its belly,' said Sharon, 'and as a worm you shall serve me, the lowliest of my lieutenants.'

And Bleary did reply, 'That's *luptenants*, O Evil One.'

And Sharon did say, 'Shut up.'

And Bleary did say, 'Certainly, O Dark Lord.'

## *Of the Death of King Gondor in Battle*

Guided by the inside knowledge of Bleary, Sharon was able to slip his troops past the defences of Elves, if not those of Men. And one night, when the moon was one-dimensional rather than two- and the stars seemed more distant than usual, a troop of Orks came silently out of the hills and attacked the elvish city of Twinned-with-Elfton.

King Gondor was asleep, and yet he roused himself quickly and prudently and strapped on his armour. And though many Elves were slain in their sleep, yet many Elves did pull swords from under their pillows or from specially constructed sword-stands beside their beds, and battle the insurgents.

For Elves are fierce fighters, and do not easily lose heart; and though the assault had the benefit of surprise yet did it falter as the Elves rallied themselves. They pushed the Orks back and to the outskirts of the city, and as dawn began to smooth away the darkness from the sky they had formed phalanxes and the Orks were in disarray.

Seeing, from his high place, that the battle was

going badly, Sharon summoned a hideous Baldtrog from his cave; and this great lumbering creature lumbered into the elven city, reducing many of the wooden houses to mere lumber with his great lumbering club. And the sunlight reflected from his hideous bald head did affright many Elves, and frighten them too. And seeing the confusion of their enemies the Orks did re-muster and assault again.

And King Gondor did cry, 'Let us not be down-hearted! Let us attack, but prudently!' And he led the charge, although with a fitting caution, and when the conditions of battle were right, and drove the Baldtrog back to the Stream Inkcold. And finally the Orks fled through the cold waters, and the Baldtrog, getting water on his bald head, did start to cry, and it seemed that victory would belong to the Elves. But at the last moment of the fight, an arrow pierced Gondor's body, and though the wound was not fatal the poison upon the arrowhead was.

The last moments of Gondor the Brave are recorded in the 'Ballad of The Last Moments of Gondor the Brave', still sung amongst the Elves to this day, unless they can think of something better to sing.

That day did Gondor, called 'The Brave'
  Get swatted by an arrow
Which stuck him in an early grave
  By sticking in his marrow.

At first he said, 'We must attack
  We must attack right now!'
But later he did say 'Alack'
  And also 'Urgh' and 'Ow'.

He led the elves in battle's press
  With awe-inspiring bellow
But now, as good as we can guess
  His bones have gone all yellow.

Laid low by his arch-enemy
  It's a coffin he's interred in;
His skin has gone all parchmenty
  And 'RIP''s his wording.

Poor Gondor! For Gondor, once 'the Bold'
Is now 'Gondor the Covered-in-mould'.
Gondor! Our once delicious king,
Is now a deliquescing thing.

Oh Gondor's lost his majesty,
And Gondor's lost his honour,
And Gondor's lost his middle d
For Gondor is a goner.

> *Oh no!*
> *An orkish arrow thwacks a tush.*
>   *Alas!*
> *'Tis Gondor's gluteus maximus.*
>   *Beware!*
> *An orkish warrior hacks him as*
> *He staggers from the strife.*
>   *Bewail!*
> *Just as French bread lacks houmous*
> *So Gondor lacks all life.*
>
> *He lies upon the grass*
> *With an arrow in his*
> *Body.*

The Orks were scattered to the hills, and hunting parties hunted them down. Party, here, is not supposed to suggest any kind of dancing, drinking or letting down of hair; these were very grim hunting parties indeed.

Gondor the Brownie was burnt upon a pyre; and his people mourned him for three days and three nights. And a new monarch was crowned, Queen Eve the Elven, daughter of Gondor and inheritor of the tainted line of King Bleary.

But because the Elves had fought the Orks alone,

an estrangement grew between the Elves and the Men. The Elves did say, 'Where were you lot, eh? Fine bloody alliance this turned out to be. Here it was, all kicking off, and you decided to have a bloody lie-in.' And the Men did reply, 'They attacked in the middle of the night! It was a surprise attack! How were we supposed to know?' And the Elves did say, 'You didn't exactly *fall over yourselves* rushing to help us when you did hear about it, did you?' And Men did say, 'Well, if you feel that way about it, maybe we'd be better off without an alliance.' And the Elves did say, 'Suits us.' And Men did say, 'Fine.' And Elves did say, 'Fine.'

So it was that the great alliance of Men and Elves fell into desuetude. And Queen Eve Attim, of the line of Arthur-Brick,[18] did vow: 'Nevermore shall my line have dealing with mortal Men.' And this vow caused great trouble in after times.

---

18   This noble elvish line of princes and princesses were so called because they combined the wisdom and courage of the fabled King Arthur with the strength and buildability of a brick. Apparently. And – before you say anything – yes, there *was* a mythological figure called Arthur in the traditions of Upper Middle Earth, just as there was in our world. Just one of those strange coincidences of names, that's all.

# Of Belend and Lüthwoman

## The First Part of the
## Tale of Belend and Lüthwoman

At this time the kings of Men were drawn from the royal house of Prorn. King Prorn the Mighty ruled seventy years and he ruled wisely and well; but he was slain eventually in the Battle of Nirhastings, pierced by many orkish arrows.

His son, King Prorn II, inherited the throne, and he also ruled wisely for many years, but died at last, as is the fate of all Men. Historians disagree about how he met his end: some say that he died battling a monstrous Baldtrog; some that he was slain by an Ork raiding party; some that he led an assault against Sharon and was burnt up by lava on the slopes of Mount Dumb; and some that he died at home, straining at stool. He was succeeded in his turn by King Prorn III, known as the Grrreat.

Now the sons of Prorn III were Stronginthearm, who grew to manhood strong in the arm; and

Braveface, who grew to manhood with the bravest face in all of the realms of Men. No terror could frighten his face, no debilitating or demoralising emotion could cause his lip to crumple or his eyes to moisten up. And the third son of King Prorn was Belend, who grew to manhood with a certain impressive attribute, into which we shall not, at the present time and in the present company, go.

Belend was a solitary soul, who spent much of his time in the woods and amongst wild animals, although not in a, you know, *funny* way; nothing odd, just a healthy, manly enjoyment of the outdoors, fresh air, a good hike, the company of big hairy bears, and so on. And he grew to full manhood, and an extremely full manhood it was too, if you know what I mean. And one day he was walking in early autumn amongst the trees of Taur-en-Ferno, with their flame-red leaves and pollen blowing off the heads of oaks like smoke.

Now, Queen Eve Arthur-Brick Attim III had one child, and this was the beautiful Lüthwoman. And one day she went wandering in the woods singing songs, swimming naked in the pools, and doing all that kind of woodland thing.

And Lüthwoman was fairer than all the fair, well-formed, elegant, light-footed and fair, or did I say that already. Anyway, she was a princess of the Elvish race of outstanding natural beauty. And Belend, seeing her, fell in love with her immediately and without delay; and approached her chivalrously and got into conversation with her. And the two of them wandered amongst the trees, talking and getting to know one another; and the longer they talked the more Lüthwoman found herself drawn to Belend. For he was handsome and courteous, and as he told her tales of his many adventures, fighting Orks, travelling in the woods of the north, and befriending the wild animals she was favourably impressed.

She said, 'Belend, you are the throngetht and bravetht of the thonth of Men.'

To which Belend replied, after a short pause, 'You what?'

'Oh Belend,' gasped Lüthwoman, flinging herself upon him, 'My paththion for you ith a thrange and overwhelming thing! Though you be mortal and I a printheth of the elvith rathe, yet mutht I embrathe you! Take me in your throng armth and kith me. Kith me! Kith me!'

And Belend replied, 'No, didn't catch any of that.' But, being no fool, he did not spurn the physical advances of so beautiful a woman, and he kithed her long and hard.

❋

The love between Belend and Lüthwoman was a mighty love, a passionate and majestic love; and after a twenty-minute rest it was a passionate and majestic love a second time. And they resolved, she and he, that they must be married.

But there had never been a marriage between an Elvish woman and a Mannish boy; no, nor between an Elvish lad and a Mannish lady.[19] No, nay, never, nonaynever not once had elf mated with aught else but elf and mortal with aught else but mortal,[20] and that had always been the way it was. But the love between Belend and Lüthwoman broke through these barriers. It was Romeo and Juliet, it was Starsky and Hutch, it was Scooby Doo and Shaggy; it was a love that shattered preconceptions and flew in the face of society's prejudices, yea, veritably flew in society's-prejudice's face like a moth flapping and making society's-prejudice flap its hands around its face and go 'Urgh! Get off!'

---

19  I don't mean a lady with, you know, a moustache or anything like that. I mean a human woman. But you had already worked that out, hadn't you?

20  Nor ork with aught but ork, nor ort with aught but ort, but that's a different matter.

And Belend came to the Elven Queen Eve, of the Eleven Elves of the Evening; and did say, 'Um, ah, don't mean to butt in, um, sorry to,' for he was rather embarrassed and, not being in the habit of talking with royalty, he didn't know what to say. So he cleared his throat, and thought to himself 'Here goes' and said: 'I wonder if I might have an audience, ma'am.' But instead of saying 'ma'am' as he intended, he was so nervous that he sort of coughed or barked halfway through the word, saying 'ma-akh!-akh!'

And Queen Eve the Elven was not impressed.

She was sitting on her silver throne, at the head of her great hall, and the benches to the left and right were filled with the noblest and handsomest of the Elvish princes and princesses, who revered her as the inheritor of the line of Bleary and Gondor.

'What is it, mortal?' she asked. 'For never in many long years has one of the sons of Men dared to enter the halls of the Elven Queen. Know ye not that our onetime alliance has fallen to desuetude?'

'To what?' asked Belend.

'Desuetude.'

'Ah,' said Belend, nodding and going for an 'of course I understand what that word means' expression on his face. 'Anyway, I really fancy your daughter.'

And Queen Eve was astonished and astonied, as well as being astied and a'ed.

'Silence!' she cried. 'Insolent mortal!'

'Sorry,' said Belend, reddening, and standing awkwardly with one foot resting upon the other. 'It's just—'

'For know this,' cried Eve, lifting her arms for a more properly melodramatic effect, 'I am Queen of the Elves. I have taken a vow that neither I nor any of my line shall have anything to do with the sons of Men!'

'Right,' said Belend. 'Well that's a bit awkward, you see, because I was rather hoping that Lüthwoman and I could get married.'

'Marry her!' cried Queen Eve, in amazement and scorn.

'She and I are in love.'

At this Queen Eve laughed. 'Men know nothing of love! Only Elves have the capacity for love: in Men it is merely lust, sentiment, habit and self-delusion. For how could it be otherwise? For Elves endure, and so their love endures; but Men wither and fade, die and pass into nothingness, and so their love is fickle.'

'Nevertheless,' said Belend growing more confident, 'I love her, and she loves me; and we wish to marry.'

'Impossible! I shall never permit it.'

And Belend did shuffle about a bit on the smooth marble flags of the elven hall, and look about him at the rows of hostile faces. And he did say, 'Oh go on.'

And Queen Eve laughed loud and contemptuously; and her nobles, and princes, and princesses laughed, following the lead of their monarch. And Belend did blush redder still, faced with the derision of these haughty elven lords and ladies.

'I say,' he said. 'This isn't very courteous of you.'

'Never in my reign,' said Queen Eve, with a curl to her lips, 'has any mortal Man dared such boldness.'

'I love her, and she loves me,' said Belend a second time. 'I ask your blessing upon our union.'

'Blessing! Rather a curse. I say you shall not marry my daughter.'

'Be careful,' said Belend, growing bolder. 'Not lightly are the curses of Elves uttered, and easily do they go astray in the wide world. I say I will marry your daughter Lüthwoman, and so says she. Shall my word come into conflict with your word? Say again.'

'I am Queen of the Elves of Upper Middle Earth, ageless and deathless; you are mortal Man,' said Eve. 'Should your word and mine come into conflict, yours would shatter as glass and mine prove adamantine.

My own life will wither and die before my word is broken. But do you speak truly when you say my daughter has chosen you over a noble Elvish prince?'

'She has.'

Eve shook her head. 'It cannot be.'

'Why not? I am worthy,' said Belend, growing bolder still.

'Can you prove such worth?' asked the Queen. 'I say you cannot – it is beyond the power of any Man.'

'Not beyond *my* power, lady,' Belend boasted.

'Very well, Belend son of Prorn,' said Eve, laughing again though not kindly. 'So be it. I lay a task upon you. Fetch me the Sellāmi that Sharon hoards in his fastness in the dead land of Moider! – Bring me that treasure of Emu, which has fallen into the grasp of evil to our cost, and you shall have the hand of my daughter in marriage.'

And the lordlings and ladylings of Elfland did laugh at this task, for it seemed to them impossible to achieve such a quest. But Belend gathered himself up to his full height, five foot ten and three-quarters, and did say, as gravely as he could, 'I shall do this thing, my lady, and after it is done I shall claim what you have promised me.'

And Belend left the Halls of the Elves, to travel, as

all thought, to his certain death. And none who saw him leave expected to see him alive again.

## The Second Part of the
## Tale of Belend and Lüthwoman

And when Lüthwoman heard what task had been set upon her beloved Belend she wept, and he comforted her in his special way, which stopped her weeping but not her cries. And after this the two of them resolved to embark on this perilous quest together. 'For,' said Belend, 'Two heads, like two breasts, are better than one.'

And Lüthwoman did say, 'Cheeky!' and make as if to slap him, but did not really slap him, it being a feint, comical play-acting of a pretend outrage rather than an actual assault.

And they did kiss once more, and caress, and make cooing noises, and call one another 'snooglums' and 'wiggly-pig' and 'jonny-tommy' and such like. And any persons that overheard them in this exchange did desire to throw up, frankly.

So it was that, one bright morning, Belend and Lüthwoman rode out together from the yellow-green spring leaves of Taur-Ea-Dorpants, and along the bridle path that they hoped would lead to a bridal path, and thence to an unbridled passion, and similar puns upon the word 'bridle' too numerous and too groany to list here.

'But,' said Lüthwoman, 'how thall we protheed? For Moidor! ith many leagueth from here, and there are hordeth of Orkth and other uglieth between uth and the throne of Tharon, Lord of Evil, Lidleth Eye that ever watcheth our advanthe. And the Thellāmi of Emu ith his motht preciouth pothethion, the object from which hith magical power largely deriveth – and none knowth in which guarded room or locked thafekeep he holdth it.'

To which Belend replied, 'Right, insofar as I understood any of that, I *think* you're asking about how we're actually going to go about grabbing this Sellāmi thing, yeah?'

And Lüthwoman nodded.

'Oh,' Belend said airily. 'I'm sure something'll come up.'

And they travelled for many days, south and east and slept at night under the far off stars, lying in one another's arms for warmth. On the third day they came to the mighty River Raver.

Now, the River Raver is the widest and wildest of

all the rivers of Upper Middle Earth. It gallops through its sharp-cut banks faster than the fleetest horses; and it is deep and cold, for its waters flow straight and hard from the frozen peaks of the Blue-joke Mountains, the Ered Loonpants. It is a league wide at its narrowest, and no bridge crosses it; and along its length are many waterfalls and stone-jagged tumbles. And no swimmer, mortal or elf, had ever gone into these waters and reached the far side.

Here Belend and Lüthwoman stopped for a day and a night, for they could not see how to cross the foaming torrent. Belend constructed a boat from leaves, which he stitched together with strands of grass. It was just about large enough for two, and it took the shape of a hollowed-out avocado skin. But when Lüthwoman looked at it she said, 'If you think I'm getting into *that* to croth the mighty river, you're very much mithtaken.'

And Belend did reply, 'Hey I understood all of that! I'm definitely getting better at understanding you.'

And looking again at his leaf/grass construction, he had to agree with her that it was pretty flimsy-looking, actually. So they did not attempt to cross the river that day, and slept on its banks that night.

The following morning the song of dawn birds rose

like flute music over the drone of rushing waters, and the sun was young and bright in a pale sky. Belend and Lüthwoman departed from their path. They made their way along the northern bank of the River Raver. After a day's trek their ears became weary of the incessant roar of the river, which grew almost as a great weight upon them, heavier with each hour. And Belend craved silence, and the peace of a forest glade; and Lüthwoman craved warmth, and air dry with midday sunshine, for her clothes and hair were wet with the spray that swirled from the water like smoke at its many rapids, waterfalls and hollows. The very air was damp and cold.

Their hearts misgave.

And Belend did say, although he had to yell for his voice to be heard above the shout of the river, 'Shall we return to Taur-ea-dorpants? Shall I take you back to Elftonjon and face the scorn of your mother? For I fear we shall never cross this great river.'

And Lüthwoman did reply, speaking shrilly in her attempt to raise the volume of her words above that of the flowing water, 'Thith eth*peth*ial thummit of thircumthtanthes ith thuch that thlinking back to the foretht ith thtrark impothible, or tho it theemth to me.'

Belend looked puzzled momentarily, and then he did grin exaggeratedly, and nod, and say, 'Yes, yes, quite right', as if he understood any of this.

They slept another night beside the titanic growl of the river, and the sound of it insinuated into their dreams and made them uneasy; and Belend dreamt that he stood before a great crowd who jeered and yelled; and Lüthwoman dreamt that she moved amongst innumerable lowing cattle of gigantic size.

In the morning Belend tried to catch fish with a line from one overhanging crag of the riverbank; but the fish of the River Raver are swift-moving and their thoughts are cold as the water, and few are attracted by a fisherman's lure. And so the two went hungry and walked east, always hoping that as they moved upriver it might grow less fierce, or flow more navigably, or that they might come to shallows or a bridge. But they did not.

And in the evening, sore and weary, and hungry, they came to a glade of conifers. And within this wood they chanced upon a house, little more than a hovel, made of whole timbers and roofed with a thatch of fir-sprigs. And they hallooed at this door, and said 'Anybody home?' and 'Hello?', which word is more usually a greeting than a question although they used it in the form of a question on this occasion.

Now, inside this dwelling lived a being of great age and great wisdom; and she had many names: she was called Witch?, or Dot, or to those who were fond of her, Auntie Dot: although, in the original language of the making of the world, her name had been at first *Punctus*. And she came out of her hut as a crone, very aged although her eyes were bright: it was as a crone that she had been first made, for she stood at the end of things. She smiled at her visitors.

'My lady,' said Lüthwoman, 'can you give uth your aid?'

'We have travelled far and are hungry,' said Belend. 'We are sorry to trouble you.'

'Young lovers,' said Witch?, 'you are welcome. I know you, Belend, and you also Lüthwoman, most beautiful of the daughters of Elves. And I know all about your quest.'

Belend and Lüthwoman were amazed; and Belend asked: 'Are you a witch?'

'I am Witch?'

'That's what I asked.'

'No,' said Witch? 'That is my name. Witch? – with a question mark at the end like that.'

'What – Witch??'

'Witch?'

'That's what I was asking you.'

'I was confirming what you said.'

'Dame Witch?' said Belend. 'I am confused. I have never before heard that names might have question marks at the end of them.'

And Witch? cackled at this.[21] 'Punctuation is my being, children. For in the beginning of things, the world was made as a beautiful though formless thing, because it derived from the affecting but insufficiently descriptive song of Emu. And the four great Dragons of Making did fly through the unformed world and did *speak* the world we see into existence – the sky and sea, the mountains and the rivers; and later Emu's angels came and spoke other words, speaking the fields and birds, the forests and animals into being. The world around us is a sentence, named into being. But a sentence must end with a punctuation point, or it will unravel; and so I was spoken into being: and so it is that I am the oldest of this world's created beings. And my function is crucial, for without me the sentence as a whole would not make sense.'

Belend was amazed to hear this. 'And so,' he asked, 'great mother, what manner of punctuation point are you?'

---

21   She wasn't laughing. This was a sort of cough that afflicted her, 'cak! cak! cak!'.

And Witch? did smile. 'To know that,' she said, mysteriously, 'is to understand the nature of existence. Such knowledge comes only with great effort, my children, and cannot be simply given away to all who pass and think to frame the question.'

'Well,' said Belend, pondering for a moment. 'It's either going to be a full stop, or a question mark, isn't it?'

'Or a colon?' essayed Lüthwoman.

'Well, a colon doesn't really end a sentence, does it?' countered Belend. 'No, I think it has to be a question mark or a full stop. Or perhaps an exclamation mark. Unless the sentence of the world ends with a dash like an experimental poem – and I don't think that sounds right.'

'You are wiser than first impressions might suggest,' said Witch?.

'Does the fact that you are known as Witch? mean that your nature is that of a question mark?' Belend asked the old woman.

'Not necessarily,' she replied. 'For I am also known as Aunt Dot, to some.'

Belend thought about it. 'It seems to me, great mother, that you are a question mark for all that; because I would prefer to believe that the world finishes in an open-ended manner, and that when it does end it will be answered in some way. If it ends only with a full point, then it is a closed thing and a limited thing; and I would prefer to believe that it is open.'

'Sir Belend,' said Witch?, 'you speak well, and what you say may be true or it may be not. Although there is a danger for anyone in shaping your understanding of the world around your preferences – for the world is not necessarily what you wish it to be. But I will say this: because of who and what I am, I live at the end of things, looking back. And so it is I know many things: I know your natures and your hopes, and I know the powers that oppose you – and they are mighty and terrible.'

'Can you help uth?' asked Lüthwoman, in a quavery voice, which is to say, crisply.

In reply Witch? smiled, and invited them inside her house for some tea.

Inside was dark, close and smoky; and yet a bright fire burnt in a flagstone grate, and there were tree-stump stools and a low table. And Aunt Dot the Witch? fed her guests with honeyed bread and fresh-brewed tea.

'So, my children,' she said, when they had supped their fill. 'You are hoping to cross the great river?'

'We must make our way to Moider! to confront the evil Sharon and regain the Sellāmi of Emu which was stolen. For only by doing so can we marry.'

'And it is marriage you wish?'

'It is.'

'Sharon is very old and powerful, and full of evil,' said Aunt Dot, gazing into her turf fire. 'His magic is a strong magic. But I am older, and my magic is stronger still.'

'Will you help us, great mother?' asked Belend in an agony of hope.

'Sir Belend,' said the crone, smiling. And the ridges and grooves of her aged face glistened in the firelight. 'All things are written into the great sentence of the world, all things for good or evil. I can change neither the letters nor their order.'

'It mutht,' said Lüthwoman, 'be a pretty long and complicated thententhe, all in all.'

'Oh, it is, Princess Lüthwoman,' said the crone. 'And few understand it. Even Sharon does not – at least not entirely, although he *thinks* he does.'

'But you understand it?' asked Belend.

To this Dame Dot only smiled.

'Great mother,' said Belend, humbly. 'I do not understand. Since you are so great and so powerful, why do you not claim this world as your own, and rule it in great majesty and state? – instead of living here as you do, in this small hut of wood thatched with fir-sprigs?'

'Don't you like my house?' asked Dame Dot.

'Oh no-no-no,' said Belend, hastily, for he had enough wit to know that it does not do to offend a witch. 'It's lovely, really lovely. Very nice. Rustic. Very rustic. Compact and bijou. It has,' he added, searching hurriedly for the right words 'um, tremendous charm and simplicity.'

'I actually *prefer* the dark, window-free look, mythelf,' said Lüthwoman, nodding along energetically with what her lover was saying.

Dame Dot seemed amused at this, and poked the fire with a charred lump of wood. 'To answer your question, Sir Belend,' she said. 'There are those who have wisdom, and there are those who have power. And then there are those who have power *and* wisdom, and having both means being wise enough to know that power is a poisoned sweetmeat. You ask me if I will help you reach Sharon and recover the Sellāmi. I can help you. But only if you know the magic charm that will compel my help.'

She looked inscrutably at them, and then inscrutably at the fire. And the fire looked back inscrutably at her, although Belend and Lüthwoman looked not inscrutable but alive with hope and anxiety.

And Belend did rack his brains for all the magic words and charms he had ever heard, and all the stories of witches his wetnurse had ever told him, to try and think what form of words might compel so magical a creature to help them. And the longer he thought the more confused his thoughts became, for he had no magic in him, and was not wise in magic lore.

But Lüthwoman spoke. 'Aunt Dot will you help uth,' she said, '*pleathe*?'

And this was indeed the magic word. 'Yeah, alright,' said the witch.

The crone got to her feet and shuffled across her rush-strewn floor to a rude wooden box in the corner of her hovel. This she opened, whereupon its rusty hinges made a rude noise, for it was a rude box. She took out something wrapped in cloth, and brought it over to Belend and Lüthwoman.

'You have many perils before you, and even if you achieve your end your perils will not be over,' she said. 'Take this,' and she handed Belend a small square of stiff parchment. And upon the parchment was written: '*Get ye Gone fro Gaol*'.

'What does this do?' Belend asked.

'I'd have thought it was obvious,' returned the crone, a little crossly, as if Belend's slowness of mind annoyed her. 'Just you stick that in your pocket or pouch for now. And you, my lady, take these.'

And from the cloth she took three small things, each no larger than a knucklebone. These she gave to Lüthwoman. And looking closely at them, Lüthwoman thought them the dried husks of insect bodies, or the fossilised cocoons of some locust or cricket-type thing.

'These,' said Witch?, 'before you start nagging me with questions, are Bugs of Truth. Very useful creatures. They are inert in the presence of truth, wrapped into their shells as you see; but they feed upon *untruths* – and in the presence of an untruth, they will come to life and flight, and devour the lie as it flies. But pay attention: each will only eat one untruth – after that they fly away, burrow into the ground, digest the lie, and produce an egg, a process which takes twelve years. So it is that they are precious, and rare, and I'd recommend you not to waste them. Carry them with you – but I warn you, if either of you utters a lie, they will burst to fluttering life in your pockets and you will lose them.'

'What happens when they devour the lie?' asked

Belend, who was far from clear on the point of these strange beasts.

'The speaker's words are turned from untruth to truth of course!' snapped the witch. 'You're not very with it, are you? Now, off you go, off you go, get on with your quest thingie and leave an old woman to her bingo and Battenberg.'

Belend and Lüthwoman thanked the crone long and sincerely. 'But,' said Belend, tentatively, for he was aware of the risk of outstaying their welcome, 'we cannot cross the mighty River Raver, so how can we come to Moider!?'

The crone went '*tch!*' and shook her head, but she spoke kindly. 'Alright, alright. Come outside.'

And they came out of the hovel into the glade, and the roaring of the river was loud in their ears again, and gnats swirled in the air like pollen, and the air smelt of pine and turf and woodsmoke. Behind the hut was a woodpile upon which were two leather saddles; they were slim saddles, without stirrups, but they were beautiful, for they were decorated with elegant swirled patterns. 'Take these,' said the crone, and even though she spoke quietly Belend and Lüthwoman could understand her perfectly despite the roar of the river.

'What shall we do with them?'

'Take them to the river's edge,' said the crone, turning away from them to go back inside her hut. 'Saddle the horses you find there, and you will be able to ride across the river.'

They thanked the crone with all their hearts, and left her glade carrying the gifts she had given them, and made their way down to the riverside.

## The Third Part of the Tale of Belend and Lüthwoman

So Belend and Lüthwoman returned to the River Raver. But at the river's edge they found no horses, and though Belend searched all the fields and copses about they found none, nor any trace that horse ever came so far south.

And they thought they would return to the crone's hut and ask her advice; but although they retraced their steps through the dewy grass, and though they found the glade again, yet they could find within it no trace of the crone's hut, or the crone herself. And by searching fruitlessly they wasted many hours, until finally Belend said: 'I think she is only to be found when she chooses to be found; for she is a creature of great and tricksy magic. We will not find her hut, howsoever long we look, unless she herself wishes it.'

So they went back down to the river's margin, and sat there. It began to rain, gently at first, and then with more force. Belend and Lüthwoman huddled together under a riverside tree, even though it gave them but poor shelter; and they watched the rain making stubble on the river's rapid surface, and they listened to the grass hissing under the rain.

Away to the west were the dragon-sculpted peaks of the Ered Loonpants, enormous, overstriding the horizon. The two lovers stared at the distant mountains through the drizzly air, and could see that a mighty storm was playing amid the purple-white peaks. Clouds black as night-sky were snagged on the summits like billowing robes in the strong wind. They blurred the mountains with torrents of rain, and stitched peak to peak with threads of lightning.

'If that storm moves from the mountains west,' said Belend, speaking the thought that was in both their hearts, 'then we will be drenched.'

'Or worthe,' said Lüthwoman, looking at the spate; for the river was swollen with rain and rode high against its banks. 'If it floodth . . .'

And Belend and Lüthwoman held one another more tightly, and wondered what to do.

❀

The storm seemed to grow less, and after a little while the rain lifted and sunshine fell instead of water. Belend and Lüthwoman stood and looked about them, feeling their hearts lighter. And in the tree above them a bird chirruped over and over, like a squeaky wheel.

Belend shielded his eyes with his hands and looked to the mountains on the horizon; and his heart grew heavy again. For the storm was still playing hugely about the peaks of the Ered Loon-pants. Grape-coloured clouds were piling higher and higher upon them, throwing strands of lightning at the mountains, and washing them with heavy rains. And as Belend looked, he saw avalanches; and though they were so distant they looked like shards falling from chalk, yet he knew they were truly vast quantities of snow tumbling down the mountain, to fall into the cold lakes at the base of the mounts from which the River Raver flowed.

And as he watched, he saw a bulge of water move, seemingly slowly in the great distance, down the higher reaches of the river. And he knew the mighty river was breaking its banks in a vast spate. 'Lüth-woman,' he said, taking hold of her. 'The river is flooding, as you feared. The floodwaters will reach us in a short while; and the time is too short for us to escape. Even if we were to climb this tree, it would be swallowed by the angry waters, torn roots and all from the ground and broken in the fury of the flood.'

'Mutht we, then, die?' asked Lüthwoman.

'If we must,' said Belend, 'then I am glad to die with you. For in death we shall not be divided, and my dearest wish is to remain with you, unsundered, forever. For your mother swore that she could never consent to our marriage; and I swore regardless that we would always be together. And now it seems to me that Fate has found a way for our two oaths to hold, neither being broken, and neither conflicting with the other. For although no ceremony has joined us, yet death will join us; and although your mother has still not consented to our marriage yet shall we always be together.'

And he wept, and Lüthwoman drew him closer to her. They could both hear, above the noise of the rushing waters, a deeper thrum, as the front of the spate drew closer to them.

'We must clutch one another tightly,' said Belend, 'so that even when we drown our bodies are joined.'

'And mutht we then drown?' asked Lüthwoman in fear.

Belend replied: 'We cannot escape.'

But as he spoke the words a Bug of Truth came to life in Lüthwoman's pocket, and struggled against the cloth. It flew out into the air and devoured Belend's words as he spoke them, such that – as much to his surprise as to hers – he found himself saying 'We shall never drown, you and I, for such is not our fate.'

And the Bug flew into the high air and was carried on the winds to the west.

'I don't underthtand,' said Lüthwoman. 'You thaid the flood was inethcapable. Tho why do you now thay that it ith not our fate to drown?'

Belend looked at her with a wild surmise, his eyes bright. 'I thought to say that we must drown,' he said. 'But a Bug of Truth took my words from the air! I must, inadvertently, have spoken an untruth when I said we must drown. Can it be that we will survive? But how?'

And at that moment, with a roar that shook the trees, the floodwaters raced round the river's bend. Belend saw the foaming whitecaps at the wave front, and he suddenly understood. 'Quick!' he cried. 'Take up the witch's saddles – for there,' he pointed, 'are the horses we must ride across the river!'

Lüthwoman's hands had only just grasped her

saddle, holding it before her, when the wall of water struck. She cried in fear, and Belend did so too: but the flood flung them high in the air, clear of the water, and as they came down their saddles fastened to the surging backbones of foam of the river. Lüthwoman, agile and elven, pulled herself round and settled gracefully into her saddle even as it twisted and shook on the river's back; and although Belend was clumsier and tumbled back into the water, yet his arms were strong and he did not let go of the magic leather. And he was able to haul himself upwards and pull himself onto the saddle, such that he too was sitting astride the river's spate. And in this fashion they clung to the pommels, and rode the bucking waters.

## The Fourth Part of the Tale of Belend and Lüthwoman

And so Belend and Lüthwoman rode the flooding River Raver, flying gloriously past the landscapes of lower Blearyland. And sunlight smashed a thousand rainbows from the foaming spray all around them; and joy lifted their hearts.

For some time they rode the river west; and

Belend began to worry that they would be swept out to sea before the flood abated. But shortly the river widened, and turned to the south, and here the flood burst its banks completely, and Belend and Lüth-woman were carried swiftly over the fields of the South.

And fast as eagles they came to the low hills that mark the beginnings of Moider! Here there was a bend in the hills upon which Sharon had encamped a great army of Orks, and it was called 'Ork-knee' because it somewhat resembled a knee, and because Orks lived there. These Orks were placed there by Sharon to guard the northern approaches of his kingdom.

When they saw the approaching floodwaters they abandoned their posts and fled; but the fastest legs cannot match the speed of floodwater, and they were caught and drowned, trampled (as it seemed to Belend and Lüthwoman) under the very hooves of their watery steeds.

It was against these hills that the floodwaters spent themselves, ebbing and dissipating into numerous pools and marshy land. And Belend and Lüthwoman were lowered to the ground, until they had been deposited on the splashy turf. They found each other and embraced, and then sploshed through the knee-high water until they had moved upland and into a drier area.

'We have saved ourselves many days' walking,' said Belend, 'and we have slipped past Sharon's guards. These hills grow into the mountains of Moider!, ahead; and if we press on we shall arrive at the very lair of Sharon himself, the Evil One.'

'We are near to the end of our quetht,' said Lüthwoman. 'But how thall we prevail upon Tharon when we come to him? How thall we compel him to give up the Thellāmi?'

And Belend had no answer to this question.

They made their way up into the higher ground, and the Unpleasant Mountains rose starkly before them. These mountains, bare of vegetation and black with volcanic sand, surrounded the terrible land of Moider! which Sharon had claimed as his own.

Belend and Lüthwoman thought they had seen enough water, and been drenched and chilled enough, for a lifetime; yet that night, as they huddled together in a hollow of black sand, they were thirsty, and wished for moisture.

'If we are thucthethul in our quetht . . .' Lüthwoman began.

'Thuck-what?' interrupted Belend.

'Don't be cheeky,' she said, slapping him lightly on his manly chest. 'All I'm thaying ith – if we return to Blearyland with the Thellāmi – thall we marry?'

'Of course, my darling.'

'And live together?'

'Yes; for I could no more be parted from you than parted with my own heart.'

'Where thall we live?'

'I shall build us a great house in the forest, equidistant between your home and mine. It shall be a mighty timber structure, three stories tall, with many chambers; and it shall be beside a forest lake, fringed with poplar and elm.'

The thought of this pleased Lüthwoman. 'And how will the interior be decorated?'

'The what?'

'The interior.'

'Well,' said Belend. 'I really hadn't given it much thought, to be honest. Some open pine, I suppose. Antlers over the fireplace. That sort of thing.'

'I wath thinking,' said Lüthwoman, 'cuthionth.'

'Cushions?'

'Yeth. And three piethe thuites. With throwth.'

'Srows?' said Belend, growing confused.

'No – *throw*th. And a floral pattern on the wallth. A bit of chrome in the kitchen, perhapth.'

'You'd like that?' said Belend, a little aghast.

'Oo yeth, I like a bit of chrome in my kitchen. Flowerth everywhere. And bowlth of dried blothrhom. Do you like the thought of that, my darling?'

To this Belend replied, 'Yes, my love – anything that makes you happy.' And his words provoked a flutter in Lüthwoman's dress; and in the moonlight one of the Bugs of Truth flew out. It caught Belend's words in the air, and gobbled them down, such that Belend heard himself saying instead 'It sounds so appalling that it makes me want to gouge my scalp with daggers or squeeze cacti under my armpits, anything to take my mind off the thought of it.'

And Lüthwoman leapt to her feet in outrage and hurt, crying 'Belend! How could you be tho unfeeling!'

And Belend leapt likewise, and said, 'Never mind that now! We've lost another of the Bugs of Truth – that's two down, and only one to go. Catch it, quickly – they're too precious to lose!'

But leap and grab as they might, the Bug of Truth escaped them, and flew high in the air to flutter away eastwards.

'That leaves only one Bug of Truth,' said Belend. 'We'd both better be careful not to utter anything untruthful, or we'll have none of the critters left at all.'

But Lüthwoman was still in a huff about Belend's hurtful comment; and she insisted she sleep alone in the hollow of black sand, and that Belend sleep 'over there' on top of the mound of sand, and added that 'if he thought he wath getting any tonight' then he had 'another thing coming'.

In the morning they were reduced to licking the dew from the bald rocks of the Unpleasant Mountains. And they trekked on, and made their way towards a gap between two peaks. 'On the far side of that,' Belend said, 'is Cirith Connoli, the tower in which the evil Sharon resides.'

They walked all day, trudging through the dark sand, and they walked on into the cool evening; and by midnight they had passed over the shoulder of land. And on the far side they slept. And in the first light of dawn they saw before them the mighty tower of Cirith Connoli, tall and slender, like a great black stick of celery reaching into the sky. I mean, ridged and stiff like celery; not moist or sprouting little green leaves like celery. Obviously. But I just thought I'd make that absolutely clear. Wouldn't want there to be any misunderstanding.

'Perhaps,' said Belend, his throat parched and stomach empty. 'Perhaps we should have brought a sack, or something, filled with provisions, some food, a canteen of water.'

And Lüthwoman nodded. 'Well,' she said, resignedly, 'we'll know for nectht time.'

And they picked their way down the side of the Unpleasant Mountains, and approached the base of the tower.

The tower was guarded by Sharon's personal bodyguard of Orks; and a cohort was stationed at the main entrance.[22] Belend and Lüthwoman snuck up behind a great boulder and peered round the edge of this to spy out the area. 'How can we creep past those guards?' Belend asked. And after asking this question he looked around, and said, 'Lüthwoman? What do you – Lüthwoman? Where are you?'

And he looked forward and saw Lüthwoman walking in plain sight up to the guards. And he did say, 'Oh crikey,' and hurry from behind the boulder to catch her up, calling 'Lüthwoman! Wait for me!'

---

22 The Ork army operated on the following structural principle: the basic soldier was the individual Ork; above that was the pairing of ork soldiers, the 'co-ork'; above that the band of one or two dozens Orks, the 'cohort'; and finally the mass, or 'cohorde'. Occasionally Orks were sent into battle without the backup of a cohorde, which is to say 'cohordless'.

And Lüthwoman, Princess of Elves, stood proud before the gate, and said 'I am Lüthwoman of the Elveth of Taur-ea-dorpantth! Thith ith Belend of the Landth of Men. We have come to thpeak with your mathter, Tharon! Take uth to him!'

And the Orks were greatly surprised and clustered around the pair, prodding them with spears and growling in their own dialect, Orkockney. 'Wos your game? Nah! Yuravinalarf, intcha? Leave it aht!' and so on.

And they hustled Lüthwoman and Belend into the tower and dunked them in a dank dungeon. In addition to being dank this dungeon was also dark. And dinky. Here they clung to one another, and Belend asked his love 'Why did you walk up in plain sight like that?' And she replied, 'I thought it would be a good idea. Anyway, we're inthide now, aren't we?' And he did say, 'Inside a dungeon.'

Sharon kept Belend and Lüthwoman in the dungeon for three days and three nights; and he fed them only spoiled meat; and they drank only what they could scrape from the cold stone of the walls. But after a time he became curious as to why they had come, unarmed and alone save for one another, to his tower. So he had them taken from the dungeon and brought before him.

And so it was that Belend and Lüthwoman beheld the giant eyeball of Sharon; and it was a little shrunken from its glory days, but still it was a giant globe of evil. Although the white portion was rather scuffed, and bloodshot like a child's red-crayon drawing of winter trees, and dented. And he had been placed by his underlings upon a special dais.

The great Lidless Eye of Evil did laugh and say 'Whom have we here? An Elf woman and a mannish, um, Man? What brings you to my lair?'

'An age ago,' said Lüthwoman, 'you thtole the Thellámi of Emu. We have come to retrieve it from you.'

At this Sharon laughed again, heartily. Or eyebally, I suppose, if you want to be strictly literal about it. 'Indeed I did steal the Sellámi!' he crowed. 'And I have no wish to return it. Why should I? It is mine, and I relish the power it gives me. Do you see this?'

And around his spherical body Sharon wore a chain of black gold.[23] And pendent on his chain was a slice of the sacred Sellámi itself, cut from the whole Sellámi, and with a circle hollowed out from its

---

23   Which is to say, a chain made from a special form of metallic gold that looks black – not a chain made from *oil*. That would be a pretty ridiculous object. You wouldn't be able to hang anything on it, for one thing.

centre so that it could be threaded onto a chain. Lüthwoman and Belend gasped with horror when they saw it – for only a creature of the lowest evil would desecrate so sacred object as the Sellāmi by slicing a sliver from it, and then hollowing out the middle, such that it became a mere hardened circle of rind. Yet did this 'Thing' possess some of the power of the sacred Sellāmi.

'You have mutilated the Sellāmi!' cried Belend.

'Ach,' said Sharon, dismissively. 'It's only a sliver. The rest of the Sellāmi is intact; I am keeping it for my future purposes. You see, the magic of the entire Sellāmi is too *potent*, even for a being such as I – it being created by the Creator himself. Trying to use the entire Sellāmi for my magic ends was like trying to paint a three-foot-by-three-foot picture using an entire fir tree as a brush. But *this* way I wield the power of the whole artefact *in miniature*. Much more manageable. I can produce mini-artefacts chipped from the whole, fitted to this world in which we live – Upper Middle Earth is of course a lesser creation than Asdar. This slice that I wear now contains enough magic to serve my purpose; and when that magic is exhausted, I shall cut another sliver from the whole. I call this magic Thing a "Tiny Morsel", or "TM" for short.'

And Sharon laughed again with great gusto.

And Lüthwoman did shudder at the evil of Sharon; and Belend moved to comfort her, but was prevented by the milling Orks shoving him back with their weapons.

'Where ith the retht of the Thellāmi?' demanded Lüthwoman.

'Why should I tell you?' said Sharon. 'My wish now is that you be executed horribly and painfully by my Orks. What good, therefore, will the knowledge of the Sellāmi's whereabouts do you?'

'Where ith it?' pressed Lüthwoman.

'It is in a safe place,' mocked Sharon. 'In a room in my domain. This is a room with two entrances, or exits, yet not a room you would ever want to enter – for, even if you knew its location, the key to the door is your own flesh, and you would leave the room quite changed from how you entered it.'

And Belend and Lüthwoman puzzled over this riddle.

'Yet,' said Lüthwoman, 'if it ith a room in thith tower, we may yet find it.'

At this Sharon only laughed.

'Take us there!' demanded Belend. 'Take us to the Sellāmi!'

And Sharon laughed loud and long at this

presumption. 'Your bravery is matched only by your foolishness!' he declared. 'Take you to the Sellāmi? Never – you shall *never* know where it is, for the Sellāmi will be mine for ever!'

And as the Evil Lord spoke these words, the final Bug of Truth stirred in Lüthwoman's pocket, and came to life. It crawled out and flipped into the air, catching Sharon's words as they were spoken: a great lie from a great liar, yet the Bug of Truth gobbled them in flight, and Sharon instead said:

'The Sellāmi is in the belly of the Pig of Doom, which terrible creature I keep in a great pit behind the tower. I feed this beast on my enemies, and upon any Orks that displease me – they are thrown, alive and screaming, into the deep pit, and the Pig of Doom devours them with great chompings; and in the belly of this terrible creature I keep the incorruptible Sellāmi beyond the reach of my enemies.'

And the Orks were astonished that Sharon had revealed this secret, for not even his closest lieutenants had been privy to the true location of the Sellāmi. And Sharon, paranoid in his fear and possessiveness, had thought no room in his castle safe enough from theft, and so had fed the remainder of the Sellāmi to his monstrous Pig. But he was horrified at what he had said, for it had not been his intention.

'Why did I say that?' Sharon cried. 'What came over me? Curses! – but *look!* Look! A Bug of Truth! Kill it, smash it, crush it—'

And the Orks ran in circles, and flailed in the air with their weapons, hoping to slay the Bug of Truth and so please their master; but the bug was agile, and flapped out of reach; and it flew high through an open casement and flew to the north. And there, eventually, it found a pleasant field, and burrowed into the soil; for it had devoured an unusually large lie, and had within itself food for a long time.

But Sharon's rage was kindled now.

'You worms!' he cried. 'How *dare* you trick me into revealing the true location of the Sellāmi! How dare you! I had planned to kill you quickly and cleanly, here: but now instead I shall fulfil your request – I shall take you to the Sellāmi, and instead of a quick death you shall meet a terrible and painful demise at the jaws of the Pig of Doom!'

And at this news Belend did tremble, and Lüth-woman moan. Because, after all, nobody looks forward cheerily to the prospect of being eaten by a giant pig. Nobody I know, anyway.

❉

When Sharon had put the sacred Sellāmi inside the Pig of Doom he knew that the magical artefact could not be corrupted or digested inside the pig's gut: for the Sellāmi, being not of this world, cannot be consumed by it. On the contrary, he knew the Pig would hold the Sellāmi in a safe and hidden place, and that when the pig died he could cut open the pig's belly and retrieve the artefact. But he had not planned on revealing this secret place to anybody, and now he was bitter and angry.

He ordered his Orks to seize Belend and Lüthwoman, and decreed that they be cast into the great pit to be devoured by the hideous pig. And to them he said, 'Your end is fitting, for you came seeking the Sellāmi, and you shall be taken to it. Let you not, therefore, complain.'

And Belend did stand as proudly as he could, bearing in mind that he had Orks hanging off him and poking him in the small of the back with spears and so on, and replied: 'I do not complain, Lord of Darkness, for I am content to die by the side of my love.'

And Lüthwoman looked over to him and said, 'Aah, that'th thoo thweet.'

And Belend did blush a little, and look at the floor, and say, 'Well, it's true.'

And Lüthwoman said, 'I love you too, my nea-tumth-thweetumth.'

And Belend said, 'Love you, gurgly-tum.'

And Lüthwoman said, 'My little love-monkey.'

And Belend said, 'My tweaky little —'

But at this point Sharon intervened, shouting, 'Oh for heaven's *sake* throw them to the pig. Jeesh, it's enough to make even an eyeball vomit.'

So Belend and Lüthwoman were dragged down the stairs and out of the Cirith Connoli; and in the wasted land behind the tower was a great and deep pit, and at the bottom of this a monstrous pig, large as a whale, well, maybe one of the smaller breeds of whale anyway, a dolphin whale or a small killer whale or something like that. And it snuffled and grunted, and picked over the bones at the bottom of its pit, and eagerly awaited its next meal.

## The Fifth Part of the Tale of Belend and Lüthwoman

There is no Fifth Part of the Tale of Belend and Lüthwoman. There is, however, a sixth, should you still be interested.

# The Sixth Part of the Tale of Belend and Lüthwoman

And so it was that Belend and Lüthwoman were hurled into the pit of the Pig of Doom. They fell far, for the pit was deep, but their landing was cushioned by the layer of muck at the bottom of the pit, the precise nature of which was something into which they, neither of them, had any desire to enquire too closely.

Orks lined the rim of the pit, looking down, jeering and yelling; and Sharon himself stared down upon them from the top of his tall tower.

The Pig of Doom, scenting new food, came trotting over towards the newcomers; but Belend got proudly to his feet and held forth his hand in a 'halt!' posture.

'Stop!' he called. 'Pig! Before you devour us, listen to my words. For I am Belend, of the royal line of Prorn, and I have spent my life wandering the forests of my native land, befriending bears, deer and pigs wherever I have found – ow!'

And he did say 'Ow' with great force and sincerity, because the Pig of Doom had bitten off his hand and swallowed it, as a morsel.

Lüthwoman screamed, or to be precise thcreamed, to see this; and Belend fell to his knees, and clutched at his stump. And he said: 'What do you think you're *doing*? For crying out *loud*, there's plenty of time to eat us, there's really no need to be so impatient, ow, ow, *owww*.'

And the Pig of Doom heard the words. In all his long years in the deep pit, nobody had ever spoken to him as if he were a rational creature. But, as it happens, he was such a creature, very intelligent animals, pigs, actually. And he heard the words, and felt a bit sheepish, rather than his usual piggish. And he held back from devouring the rest of Belend for a little space.

'Hell's *bells*, that stings,' said Belend, trying to staunch the flow of blood from his stump by wrapping his shirt around the wound in a sort of ball of cloth. 'Ouch, ow, ow, ow, *ow*,' he added.

'Sorry,' snorted the Pig.

'Couldn't you even let me finish my *sentence*? I mean, what's the bleeding *hurry*?'

'Got a bit carried away,' said the Pig. 'Sorry. Only they usually feed me Orks, and Orks taste yucky, frankly, between you and me. I got a bit overexcited, to be honest. You look just so much tastier than my usual fare. People think I'll eat anything, and actually

I will, pretty much, but that doesn't mean I lack all sense of culinary pleasure. Quite the reverse. Actually, do you know what I really fancy?'

'What?' asked Belend, although his tone of voice implied somebody not happy with the cosmos and he spoke snappishly.

'Truffles. Oo I'd *love* a truffle right now. You got any truffles on you?'

'No,' said Belend and he looked at his partner. 'Have you got any truffles on you, dear?'

'Thorry,' said Lüthwoman. 'No.'

'Ah well,' said the Pig.

'Ith it true,' asked Lüthwoman in wonder, 'that you carry the thacred Thellāmi in your belly?'

The Pig's face assumed a pained expression. 'Yes, that's perfectly true. It's not at all comfortable, I don't mind telling you. Sharon chucked it down here a while ago, and I gobbled it down without thinking twice. But I can't seem to digest it. I can feel it as a sort of jagged lump, about here.' And he tapped one of his flanks with his left back trotter.

'Think,' said Belend, his voice faint, 'think I've got the exsanguination under control.'

'Look,' said the Pig. 'I really am sorry about the, you know, eating your hand and everything. It's just that . . .'

'Will you listen to me, Pig?' asked Belend, getting to his feet. 'Will you hear me out?' And he was much paler than he had been before.

And the Pig replied, 'Alright, I suppose that's only fair. But, just so's you know, after that I *will* have to eat you. They won't give me any more food until I do, and, well. You know. Pig's gotta eat, after all.'

'Listen to me, Pig,' said Belend, looking woozy, as if he were about to pass out. 'I possess the power to free you from this pit, and carry you far away from Moider!, into the wide forests of the north.'

'You do?'

'Yes,' said Belend. 'Forests absolutely stuffed with truffles, just lying there under the topsoil, waiting for your snout to uncover them.'

'Oo!' went the Pig, going all dreamy-faced. If you've never seen a pig's face go all dreamy then you have missed something remarkable, believe me.

'But you have to promise not to eat us,' said Belend. 'And you have to agree to come with us to the Court of Queen Eve before you get the free run of the forest. Deal?'

'Deal!' said the Pig. 'Abso-pigging-lutely. Get out of here? Truffles for life? No *question*.'

So, with Lüthwoman's help, Belend climbed up onto the hog's back. And Lüthwoman climbed up to sit in a position in front of him, and she clutched onto the Pig's ears; and Belend hooked his stumpy arm around Lüthwoman's waist. And with his good arm he brought out, from his pocket, the small rectangle of parchment, upon which was written '*Get ye Gone fro Gaol*'.

'Here,' he called. 'I play this card!' And he cast it on the floor.

And they were released from their prison; the Pig of Doom rising into the air before the astonished and angry Orks, and floating past the tall tower of Sharon like something from a nineteen-seventies album cover. And Sharon's rage was immense and terrible, but impotent; for there was nothing he could do. The Pig of Doom flew north, carrying its two passengers with it.

And the Pig said, 'Wheeeeeeh!' But not in a shrieking terrified piglet sort of way, more in a delighted, isn't-this-fun manner.

They flew over the wasted lands of the south, where floodwaters still lay in great stretches; and over the swollen torrent of the River Raver; and they flew over the southern boundaries of the great wood Taur-ea-dorpants, until they came to Elftonjon.

And the Elves were astonished to see this Pig

flying through the air, and more astonished to see it coming down to land on a stretch of turf before the margin of the forest, on the outskirts of Elfton. And they were even more astonished than this to see Lüthwoman, their princess, clamber down from the Pig's back, helping the injured Belend after her.

Messengers ran to fetch the Queen, and she was carried forth on a silver litter, and placed before the Pig; and the nobles of Elfton gathered around these ragged and wounded travellers. Yet, despite their disdain, the fabled hospitality of the Elves was not abandoned; and the new arrivals were refreshed with elf-bread, elf-honey and elf-tea. Finally the Queen spoke.

'I sent you, Belend of the tribes of Men, on a quest to retrieve the Sellāmi, and I see you took my only daughter with you into this hideous peril. Is this your love for her, that you would risk her life?'

'My love for her,' said Belend, somewhat refreshed by the elf-tea, but still weak and pale, 'is such that I cannot be parted from her.'

'Have you brought the Sellāmi? I do not see it.'

'Indeed I have brought the Sellāmi, your majesty. It is inside the belly of this Pig of Doom.'

Gasps ran through the crowd; for they were amazed and disbelieving. But the Pig, sensing that his moment had come, spoke up. 'It's true. Sharon had me imprisoned in a pit, and fed me the Sellāmi, to keep it – as he thought – safe and hidden. But this Elf and this Man discovered his secret, and freed me.'

'I asked you to bring me the Sellāmi,' said the Queen, angrily. 'And instead you have brought me a talking pig?'

'Not *instead of*, your majesty,' said Belend, proudly. '*In addition to*. You did not specify that I was to bring you only the Sellāmi and nothing else. And so I have brought you the Sellāmi *and* a pig.'

'But how am I supposed to get it *out* of the pig?'

'With respect, your majesty,' said Belend, 'that also was not something specified in your instructions when you sent me on the quest. I have fulfilled my part of the bargain, and I ask that you now fulfil yours.' And Lüthwoman did embrace him happily, and the two of them beamed smiles at the assembled Elves.

But Queen Eve was not pleased, and glowered. 'It is true,' she said, speaking slowly, 'that I said to you "bring me the Sellāmi, that treasure of Emu and you shall have the hand of my daughter in marriage". And I must be true to my word. But I also swore that you would never marry my daughter – for, you are not one jot or tittle less obnoxious to me now than you were before you went away. The thought of you and my daughter together, of you living in the same house, of you starting a family – this cannot be endured.'

And she pondered for a while; for the oath of a monarch is not lightly to be cast aside. And finally she spoke.

'I have decided: I shall keep both my oaths. Do you come to me to palter with me over the terms and conditions of the quest on which I sent you, Belend, son of Prorn? Then hearken.' And her face grew dark as a stormcloud. 'Belend the Onehanded, you yourself teach me the way I must go to preserve my oaths. You shall have the hand of my daughter in marriage, but the rest of her shall stay in Elfton with her own people.' And she called for an axeman.

And tall elf guards tore the screaming Lüthwoman away from Belend; and he was too weakened by exertion and loss of blood to fight them away. And he collapsed to the ground, sobbing in frustration and agony.

So it was that Queen Eve ordered the cutting off of the hand of her own daughter. The axeman severed her left hand with a single blow of his silver axe, and elf healers hurried to bind the wound and staunch its hurt. And Lüthwoman fell into a swoon, and was lifted aboard the Queen's litter and carried inside the town; and the crowd dispersed. And soon Belend was alone and weeping in the dirt.

And the Pig of Doom coughed discreetly, and after a while said, 'So, am I done here? Only, I thought I might wander into the – you know, the forest and have a look for truffles.' And he received no reply from Belend save his sobs, and so he departed into the depths of Taur-ea-dorpants.

And after a short space a messenger came from Queen Eve, and stood before the prone son of Prorn. 'Belend,' he said. 'I carry two things from the Queen. One is this object.'

And he threw the severed hand of Lüthwoman upon the dirt before Belend.

'The other,' he continued, 'is this speech. The Queen says she has fulfilled her obligations to you, and kept her oath. She orders you to leave this land, and never to return. You are a proscribed person. If any Elf sees you within these lands, they are to kill you on the spot. If you are still found here tomorrow at dawn the soldiers of the Queen will hunt you down and carry your severed head to the Queen. Begone – you are banished.'

Belend quietened his own tears, for he did not

wish to cry before the insolent messenger of the Queen. And he picked up the hand of his beloved, rose to his feet, and departed from those lands.

## The Seventh and Final Part of the Tale of Belend and Lüthwoman

Belend made his melancholy way north, eating mushrooms from the forest floor, and honey from beehives; and though the bees stung him in their miniature, multiple fury, yet he was heedless of that. He carried Lüthwoman's severed hand with him at all times, tucked into his shirt.

He did not return to Manly town, for his grief was too great. Instead he made his way to the great amber lake of Lothlomondwisky, and dwelt in the land of Pebles for a certain time, living with himself and with his sorrow only. And when men came to fish in the lake, Belend did not make himself known to them, but instead crossed the River Optik where it empties into the lake and crossed the stony land of Pebbles beyond. For he could not bear the company of others.

Winter came; and the wind became peevish and cold, and found the holes in Belend's clothes. And a small, chill rain fell upon him. He clad himself in the skins of rabbits he trapped, working the pelts with flints and curing them in the waters of the Loth. And he ate the flesh raw, for he could start no fire in the constant drizzle. And at all times he kept the hand of his loved woman about him: and this, being elf-flesh, did not degrade or decay, but stayed pure and white, as if carved from ivory.

And one day, when winter had lasted so long that he had almost forgotten what it was to be warm, or see flowers bloom, Belend had wandered so far as to chance upon the Standing Stones that are truly called the Dragon's Claws. For these monoliths, though they appear to sight and touch nothing more than great stones arranged in a circle, are in fact something else. The Dragon of the North, so the legend has it, carved the great Mount Ezumas-revenge with his own claws; and so mighty is this mountain that it broke the fingernails of even so vast a creature as the dragon. And the Dragon of the North shed his claws, and grew a new set; and the claws fell from on high and embedded themselves in the turf far north of Taur-en-Ferno.

Belend came to this place, and sat inside the circle. And he could sense the powerful magic of the place, for Dragons distil the greatest creative magic of any living beings. They made much of the world, and then they seeded the rocks and the mountains with life (and life that followed a complex pattern of developmental metamorphosis, I might add).

And in this place it occurred to Belend to bury the hand of Lüthwoman in the exact centre of the circle. And that night he slept over the burial site, and wept at having lost his love.

But in the morning he awoke to something strange and wondrous; for from the planted hand had grown a new Lüthwoman, whole. She was lying naked on top of the grass, with her hand tucked into the ground. And when Belend pulled her hand free of the dirt it was cold and dead as ever it had been; but the rest of this new-grown Lüthwoman was warm and quick with life.

His joy was so great it threatened to snap his own grip on life, making his heart stumble in its frantic beating, and a red mist passed before his eyes; and he embraced and embraced her, and wept, and howled his happiness to the winter sky.

It was not long, however, before he understood that although this creature possessed the physical form of his love, yet her mind was blank and her head empty: she had no speech, and made no sign of understanding. And Belend's heart fell again. It seemed to him a mockery of the fates that his Lüth-woman should be taken from him, and this empty shell given in her place.

Still he took her with him, and dressed her in rabbit skins; and she ate hungrily as a child when he gave her food, but otherwise she sat silent and pliant, or walked when he pushed her, or stopped when he stopped. And they made their way south down the western edges of Taur-en-Ferno. Hope remained in Belend's heart that this wraith might grow slowly to awareness, but many months passed and she was as blank as she had been at the beginning.

And on the west coast of Upper Middle Earth, Belend tarried. For he had decided what to do, but was uncertain whether he would be able to maintain the resolve to do what must be done. And he sat for long hours staring at the sea, with the mute simula-crum of Lüthwoman by his side. And he watched the sun setting, casting a sheen over the calm waters like a dew; and as the sun's rim kissed the edge of the horizon, and red spilt over the rippled surface of the ocean, he was resolved.

He trapped deer in the sparse woodlands of the west with snares made of creepers and the boughs of trees; and for a rude iron blade he traded the carcasses of these with fishermen who lived on the coast. This blade he sharpened on the flat stones of a coastal stream, all the time with the simulacrum of Lüthwoman watching him non-comprehending.

Then he sat beside her, and spoke to her long, explaining what he must do, and saying how sorry he was, and how he would be as kind in his cruelty as he could; but she understood nothing. And then he took his blade, and took her left arm, and cut the hand from the arm.

She cried with pain and fought him, but he held her and dressed the wound with mosses and skins. And very soon the fit passed from her, and she seemed to have forgotten the pain utterly, for she became as blank and pliable as before.

Now Belend made his way east. And his time in the wilderness, trapping animals and avoiding company, had made him cunning in the ways of the wood, expert at disguise, skilled at moving undetected. And so he led the simulacrum of Lüthwoman through the trees of Taur-ea-dorpants; and one night he crept into Elftonjon. Although discovery would have been death, yet he evaded detection, and crept about the town with the silent copy of Lüthwoman beside him.

And he made his way to the royal palace, at the heart of the town. Here, in the shadow of an eave, he left the simulacrum of Lüthwoman sitting. And he climbed the flank of the royal palace, and slipped through a casement, and stealthily returned to the side gate, opening it from the inside. And he drew the simulacrum of Lüthwoman in through the gate and brought her upstairs.

This night there was a feast in the central hall, and although servants came and went, to fetch and carry, yet were the corridors and rooms of the palace mostly empty; and Belend was able to mount the stairs unobserved, and finally he came to the door of Lüthwoman's chamber.

Here he put his hand in at the lock and opened it, and crept inside. Lüthwoman was asleep on her bed, but woke to hear his tread, and almost called out.

'Hush,' he said. 'It is I.'

And she wept to see him, and they embraced. 'But,' she said, 'it ith madneth for you to come here, for you will be killed on thight. And,' she added, fingering his shirt, 'what'th thith? Rabbit? That'th *tho* latht theathon.'

'I have come to take you with me,' said Belend.

'I have dethired nothing elthe for long monthth,' wept Lüthwoman. 'But it cannot be! My mother would never retht until I wath returned to her. It would mean war between Elveth and Men, and an army of elvith warriorth would comb the landth of Upper Middle Earth until I wath retrieved – and you would thurely die in the protheth.'

'Got that pretty much all,' said Belend, nodding, 'except for the last word. But it doesn't matter. I have a plan.'

And he went out of the room and returned with the simulacrum of Lüthwoman. And the real Lüthwoman was amazed, and examined her double in great detail.

And Belend stood looking admiringly at the two versions of the beautiful Lüthwoman standing close to one another; and he meditated on the various possibilities it presented him. But there was no time to be lost with such idle fancies; they could be discovered at any time; and so he led the simulacrum of Lüthwoman to the bed, and made her lie down; and soon she was asleep.

And Belend and Lüthwoman crept out of the palace, and out of Elfton, and fled through the woods, and never again returned to that place.

Later that night the Queen sent a messenger to summon her daughter down to the feast. And the simulacrum of Lüthwoman was brought downstairs and sat at table and ate heartily; but she would answer no question, and make no comment. And the Queen, knowing something was wrong, ended the feast in confusion, dismissing her guests, and called the finest elf doctors to the palace. They examined the simulacrum of Lüthwoman, but they did not comprehend that it was but a simulacrum, and took it for the real individual. And so they told the Queen that her daughter had lost her mind, most likely with grief at losing her lover. 'It may be, your Majesty,' they said, 'that she has lost all powers of speech, or of rational thought.'

And the Queen was greatly grieved, but try as she might she could not restore her daughter to her faculties. Over the months that followed, she tried herbs, and magic charms; she tried imploring her daughter, and hypnotising her after the manner of the Elves, but Lüthwoman remained as blank as ever. And the Queen said, 'The glory has departed from the house of Bleary, a cursed house, for now my only daughter has lost her mind in the madness of love for a mere mortal.'

Of the real Lüthwoman, one-handed, with her one-handed lover Belend, this story does not tell much more. They fled together to the north, to the pleasant meadows and copses of the land south of the River

Optik; and here Belend did build a house, and Lüth-woman did decorate it after her heart's desire. And they traded occasionally with the Men of that area, and became known to them, although not by their birth-names. And they were married, and some say they had children, but others say not.

But Queen Eve had sworn that Belend would never marry Lüthwoman, and had said also that her own life would wither and die before her word was broken. And, though unbeknownst to her, yet Belend and Lüthwoman married after all; and she did sicken and grow thin. Though an Elf and not fated for death, yet did she grow closer and closer to death.

And eventually she died: a rare fate for an Elf, to die otherwise than in battle. And she was mourned by the Elves, for she was the inheritor of the line of Bleary. But amongst the Men she was not mourned, for her story had spread through the land, and mortals called her 'Eve the Cruel' for the manner in which she had upheld her oaths.

Some amongst the Elves did say 'We should crown her daughter Queen, for she is the only remaining inheritor of the line of Bleary'. But others did say, 'Her mind has gone, and her soul lost utterly; she can never rule the Elves.' And so the

Elves fell into division and confusion, and one party separated from another party.

So ends the tale of Belend and Lüthwoman.

# Of Sharon's Dream

Now Sharon was piqued to have lost the Sellāmi. I mean, really, very, very annoyed indeed. You can understand his position, I'm sure, losing the most powerful magical artefact in creation and everything; it's bound to tick you off. He raged hard. He raged himself ragged. He railed at his Orks, slaying many. Then he raged again, or re-raged. And, having worn himself out with so much raging, and feeling weak, he reined in his rage, or de-reraged, and then he slept, for he had exhausted himself. And he slept for twenty months long, because the loss of the Sellāmi had worn him out so utterly.

As he slept he dreamt, and he saw a great shape filling the whole sky, black and purple and swirling like a stormcloud. And as he looked more closely he saw that it was a Sky Boa, a serpent of untold length and girthed with black muscles, tight to crush and destroy, and it writhed through the air like an ever-twisting band of darkness.

Now Sharon had never dreamt before, and he was terrified by the apparition. But after a little time he realised that the wraith could not harm him, and he grew bolder. 'Creature!' he called. But even though his was the voice of a Valūpac, yet it was barely a squeak in the howling gale of his dream.

'Sharon,' called the beast, and its voice was the shattering of worlds and the growl of icebergs chewing at the land. And Sharon quailed, and thought to himself, 'It is the spirit of Moregothic, slain in this world and refused entrance to the next, and so it inhabits the space between the earth and the sky in sorrow and rage.'

'Master?' said Sharon; and this was a word he had not framed in speech for an age and an age.

'Sharon,' called the apparition. And now it seemed to have a head, and its head was like a black bull except that its mouth contained sharp viper teeth of bright red; and below its neck were two strong arms, like the arms of a man, except that they ended in great talons instead of fingers; and its body tapered away over many leagues into a long tail like a huge eel. And as Sharon looked, the beast's claws were clasping its own tail, and feeding it into its own maw, and it was devouring itself. And with each bite of its colossal mouth, lightning sparked and branched away with a brightness that seared the eyes. But as Sharon gazed, this sudden brightness did not illuminate the dark, which grew more involved, minute by minute.

'Master,' called Sharon, in his dream. 'Why do you visit me in this form?'

'To warn you,' said the serpent, 'beware the promises of Dragons.'

'The promises of Dragons were your undoing, Master,' cried Sharon, full of sorrow.

'The Dragons give, but they also take. They always give as they always take. You must be ready. You must be clear before you treat with them what their price is, and you must be prepared to pay it.'

'Death was the price *you* paid,' cried Sharon.

'Ensure that the charm they weave you is watertight,' howled the serpent. 'Leave no chink in the magic. Leave no gap through which destructive fate may assail you!'

'Master!' called Sharon, in an agony of sorrow and despair and fear. And he awoke.

Never before had Sharon's servants seen his eyeball coated in the clear salty liquid in which he found himself on awakening. Nor could anybody say whence these gallons of tears had come, for though he was an eyeball, yet Sharon lacked the ducts through which tears wash the eye in other beings.

Nor could any say how he had dreamt, for he had never experienced a dream before, and the Valūpac do not dream.

Sharon contemplated the dream for a long time, and resolved to follow the advice he decided was contained within it. He could summon the Dragons, and make a binding deal with them; and he bent his cunning to the task of forming a charm that allowed no loopholes. But there was also the matter of the price to be paid, and he pondered this for a long time.

Twelve years passed after the Sellāmi was stolen from his realm; and all that time Sharon mustered a new army, vast and hideous, and armed them, and prepared his way. And, from time to time, Sharon would hear stories of a monstrous pig living in the forest of Taur-ea-dorpants in the middle of Upper Middle Earth; and he said to himself, 'That's where the Pig went.' So he resolved to steal back the Sellāmi to himself, or at the least to discover its location, for here, he thought, was a price that would purchase the Dragons' magic.

And so he marshalled a small band of his troops, and sent them north into Blearyland. His most trusted lieutenants he sent too, Bleary and Cük too.

They built ships, for they were skilled in the crafts of boatbuilding, and crossed the flooded lands of the River Raver, and so they came to the north. They did not engage in open battle with Men or Elves, for that was not their instruction; but when they came upon small groups or travellers they slew them and word spread to all the towns of the north of their doing.

And they captured Men and Elves, and tortured them, and so learned the story of Queen Eve, and how her daughter was driven to madness and blankness of mind by her love for a mortal, for so the story went. And they learnt that a monstrous Pig of Doom haunted the Forest of Taur-ea-Dorpants, and so they made their way into the forest.

And on the seventh day of searching through the trees they found the Pig, rooting at the turf to uncover truffles.

And Bleary said to his second-in-command, 'Look, there he is. You go and get him.'

And the Ork looked at the giant pig, and at his flesh-shredding teeth, and the strongly efficient action of his masticating jaws, and at the sheer *size* of the bugger, and did reply, 'Fat chance.'

'Look,' said Bleary. 'I'm giving you a *direct* order.'

'And I'm giving you a *direct* not on your nelly.'

'Do you want Sharon to be peeved?' said Bleary.

'Because, believe me, he will be peeved. He'll be very peeved indeed.'

'You want the pig,' said the Ork, in effect resigning his commission with these words, 'you go get him.' And this Ork was not sorry to leave the Orkish armies, and he travelled far, eventually setting up a smallholding, farming lemmings and selling the pelts on the outskirts of Ill-bhavior. But his subsequent life is not the concern of the present tale.

Bleary ordered the rest of his men to charge the Pig, but they were swiftly disposed of by the monster, who bit some of them in half, and batted others away with powerful sideswipes of his head, and scared others away by snorting and grunting very loudly. And the Ork raiding party withdrew in disarray.

Bleary travelled south again with the survivors, and reported what he knew to Sharon. And, as Bleary had prophesied, Sharon was peeved; and vented his anger on a couple of Orks who happened to be digging a latrine trench not far from his tower, which was bad luck for them. But after that he calmed down, and thought to himself, 'At least I know where the Pig of Doom has gone.'

## *Of Sharon's Decision to End Things Once and for All and for All*

After meditating on the situation for a long time, Sharon the Evil called Tuoni Bleary to his side, and he said to him: 'Tuoni, I have been fighting this war against so-called Goodness for ages and ages. Moreover, where most people use that phrase to mean "for forty-five minutes" or "for three months", I use it in a strictly literal sense: first age, upper second age, lower second age, third age – I've stuck it out. It's enough to try the patience of an evil saint. Well, I've decided that enough is enough.'

'Your tautologies are indeed glorious, O Evil One,' said Bleary.

'I've decided,' said Sharon, 'to end this war once and for all.'

And Bleary said, 'Good idea, O Lord. So, when you say for *once and for all*, what do you mean by "all"? – Do you mean "for all people"?'

'Yes,' said Sharon. 'End it for once and for all people. And, come to think of it, for all time.'

'So you're planning to end it once and for all and for all?'

'Exactly,' said Sharon. 'Once and for all and for all. If one is, for instance, doing a crossword, then a temporary or partial solution is simply no good. The only solution that's any use is a *final* one. Surely we can agree on that.'

And Bleary squirmed and smiled and said, 'And how will you do this thing, O Darkling? I listen.'

'To end it once and for all and for all,' said Sharon, 'I shall defeat all the forces of so-called Goodness in a mighty battle, slay their commanders and make prisoners of their followers. And I shall bind the world of Upper Middle Earth with a charm of such potency, a charm of such power-to-create, that it will hold the realm in my grasp for ever.'

'How will you frame such a spell?' asked Bleary, afraid.

'The Dragons will do it,' said Sharon.


It was spring again, and the long winter had passed, and the peoples of Upper Middle Earth felt their hearts expand with hope as the season changed. The wheat grew green in the north, and red windflowers were dotted amongst the stalks of wheat. On the meadows and downs the grass was feathery, and young figs grew white and woolly on the trees. All the green land seemed refreshed under the blue sky, washed with hurrying bright showers, and sparkling after each with sunshine anew. Men forgot for a while that there was such a thing as evil in the world, and though Elves do not forget, yet even they delighted in the warmth in the air, and sang songs beneath the chalk moon and purple sky.

And it was at this time that Sharon had himself carried to the very top of the tower of Cirith Connoli, and placed there alone on his podium. It was sunset, the sky red-gold, with olive-coloured clouds lying in layers over the western horizon. And he had about him the Thing™, in which still inhered much of the power of the Sellāmi.

Using the power of the Thing™, Sharon summoned the Dragon of the South.

And the Dragon answered his call, drawn by the Thing™. He rode the air, and pressed down upon it with wings broad as clouds; yet he brought no tempest with him as he flew, but rather he poured fluidly through the air. His eyes were green as cypress leaves, and his skin glowed dark as wine.

He circled the tower at Cirith Connoli with immense slowness. And even Sharon was afraid, but he overcame his fear.

'Dragon!' he called. 'You are the oldest and the most powerful of magic creatures in Upper Middle Earth. And yet there is an artefact older and more powerful than you – the Sellāmi, for it was created by Emu.'

And the Dragon circled the tower in the air, slowly, slowly, and said, 'I know it.'

'You shall make me a spell,' said Sharon, 'and I shall tell you where you may find the Sellāmi. None but you are mighty enough to take it from its present hiding place, and yet you do not know where it is hidden.'

And the Dragon circled the tower again in the air, and said, 'I shall do it.'

'So!' cried Sharon. 'But listen to me, Dragon. I know how you and your kind betrayed my master of old, Moregothic: for you gave him a charm of seeming strength yet at the last it betrayed him to death and extinction. This shall not be my fate. Do you hear?'

The Dragon said, 'I hear.'

'I must be lord over *all* Elves and Men, for as long as Elves and Men exist.'

The Dragon said, 'It shall be.'

'I must be invulnerable to harm.'

The Dragon said, 'It shall be.'

'I must be immortal.'

The Dragon said, 'It shall be.'

'I must be victorious in any battle.'

The Dragon said, 'It shall be.'

And Sharon demanded these four things, for he knew there were four Dragons. And he thought that there was no loophole, or ambiguity, or weakness in this charm.

The Dragon of the South said, 'These things shall come to pass when we have the Sellāmi.'

And Sharon replied: 'Agreed – all save this sliver, which I wear about me now. This I shall retain, and you will agree that my retention will not affect the spell.' The Dragon of the South reared in the air, and spread his wings so wide that they blotted out the light from the setting sun. But Sharon was not afraid: 'You shall not trick me,' he called, 'as you tricked Moregothic! Accept my terms, or get you gone.'

And the Dragon folded its wings, and flew slowly once around the tower.

'It shall be,' he said.

The land was silent, as dumb as death; no insect stirred and no wind moved. The skies were silently changing form, with the clouds forecasting night-storm; a great cloud gathered in the west, breeding thunder and lightning in its body. For this was the mightiest spell that had yet been cast in Upper Middle Earth. The hollow hills trembled, and Orks fled whimpering to their bunkers and holes.

And Sharon gloried as the tempest broke around his tower, and the lightning revealed itself in a thousand burning shards, and blue rain fell through the dusk. Far away, Men and Elves saw the conflagration on the southern horizon and wondered at such sudden and malevolent weather.

The four Dragons flew together to the middle of the world, and the wood of Taur-ea-Dorpants. They had not been to this place, singly or together, since the creation of things; but they flew there now.

And within the glades of this forest was the Pig of Doom. Tall as a house, keenly aware of its surroundings by scent and eye, this beast feared no hunter, acknowledged no predator. No forest lion or bear could dent its thick skin; no hunter's spear could harm it. It roamed where it wished, and drank from forest streams, and grubbed truffles and tubers with its shovel-like snout.

Its life was good.

But the Dragons came. Though they were vast, yet they were nimble in the air, and they swirled low over the treetops. The shade cast by their wings made the bark of the trees blue and darkened the leaves. The Pig of Doom looked up.

Now, being alone in the woodland, there was nobody with whom to speak, yet nevertheless it spoke, and said: 'Uh-oh.'

And the Dragons did gather in the sky above the Pig of Doom. And the Pig did take to its trotters in no uncertain manner, and, well, I was going to say scuttled away, but I'm not sure, on reflection, that it would be proper to describe a creature as large as a house running as fast as it can as *scuttling*. Galloping, I suppose, although that makes you think of horses, doesn't it, rather than seventy tons of mobile pig. Well, it was moving rapidly, anyway, that's what I mean to convey. Because the Pig of Doom knew that in the centre of the wide forest of Taur-ea-Dorpants was an outcrop of rock, overgrown with trees; and an opening in this led down to a deep cavern, for the world, breathed into being by the words of the Dragons, is hollow. And the Pig thought to itself, I'll lie low, in a literal sense, 'til these Dragons buzz off. Sooner I get there, he thought, the better.

And the Dragons flew through the air over the trees following him.

The Pig of Doom looked up again and saw the

shapes of the Dragons sweeping through the sky above the highest branches, and he quickened his stride. He, shall we say, *lumbered* through the trees I suppose, except that 'lumbering' implies a lumpish, ungainly, slow gait, and this pig moved with excessive rapidity. I'm beginning to think that there just isn't a word in the language to describe the extremely rapid movement of a seventy-ton pig through a forest; a state of affairs which is, I'm sure you'll agree with me, a shame. Anyway.

The Pig, casting nervous looks into the air to check on the progress of the Dragons, ran head first into a massive elm. The tree shattered into many fragments, and the Pig of Doom hurtled rump over snout, crashing into further trees in the process until it lay, stunned, in a motionless heap.

The Dragons brought themselves together in the air above the supine pig.

'Wait,' called the Pig, in a woozy voice. 'Ur, ooh, wait.'

'Pig,' called the Dragon of the South. 'We must claim the Sellāmi that is in your belly.'

'Belly!' said the Pig, struggling to get to its feet. Or to its trotters, rather. 'Belly, pah. People are so rude to pigs. If I were an Elf, or a Man, you'd say *intestine*, or *innards*, or something.'

'Nevertheless,' called the Dragons. 'The Sellāmi must be ours.'

'To be honest,' said the Pig of Doom, 'I'll not be sorry to be shot of the thing. Terrible indigestion it has caused me. Terrible – sticks into my flesh something shocking.'

'The Sellāmi is too powerful for flesh to touch,' said the Dragon of the West, 'even flesh as tough as yours, O Pig. It has corroded your innards, melted itself into your very bones.'

'Well,' said the Pig of Doom, 'that would explain the indigestion. And it would explain why I can't seem to vomit the horrid thing up. Ah well,' it said, resigning itself to its fate. 'I've had a good run, for a pig. Ate one too many Orks, perhaps, but I've certainly enjoyed the last few years, with the truffles and all.'

And he presented himself to the Dragons; and they paid tribute to his bravery, and called him, 'Some Pig'.

Then the Dragons reared in the sky and blew down with fire from all four mouths; and the Pig of Doom met his own Doom in the fiercest of conflagrations, blinded by the heat and light and breathed from existence in an instant.

The fire burnt through the Pig's flesh, and it

peeled back as a book peels its pages away in smoke when thrown onto a hearth fire. And the trees around burst to flame as brands, and a great tower of smoke rose to the air, and was bent by the wind and dispersed over the land of the east.

The Dragons stopped their fire; and below them was a great circle of black earth, smouldering and glowing in many places; and the edge of the circle was formed of flaming trees; and in the very centre of the circle was the Sellāmi, unharmed by heat and unsullied by ash.

The Dragon of the North took it in its talons, and the four Dragons flew away.

Stormclouds followed their tails, and spring rain fell on Taur-ea-dorpants, extinguishing the fires. And soon grasses grew in the scorched circle at the very heart of the forest, and out of the fertile ash came poppies and orange windflowers; but no trees ever grew in that space again.

The spell was completed; and Sharon, in his tower of Cirith Connoli, felt a great surge of strength flow through his being. And he exulted.

'The charm is complete!' he called. 'I am armed with total power, for the Dragons have promised me that I shall be lord over *all* Elves and Men, for as long as Elves and Men exist; and I am invulnerable to harm; and I am immortal; and I shall be victorious in any battle. This magic has no chink or loophole, but by the force of inevitability I shall dominate the whole of Upper Middle Earth. None shall escape.'

And he gathered together his army, and prepared to march north over the River Raver and to subdue all the peoples of Upper Middle Earth.

## *Of the Sense of Foreboding Experienced by Men and Elves*

Men and Elves watched with foreboding as the season curdled, and spring seemed to retreat. As the power passed from the Dragons to Sharon, so the sky grew bone pale, and a bleak wind came searching from the north, withering the green wheat and turning the white blossom to ice on the trees.

And King Prorn III, Lord of Men, called his advisers about him. 'Tell me why it is,' he asked them, 'that the season reverses? The land has become inhospitable; winter succeeds spring; bears and wolves prowl the woodlands, and only yesterday I slipped on some ice on my bathroom floor and barked my shin, very painful, that.'

And the royal advisers could not explain it, except that it boded ill for the lands of Men. 'Surely,' they said, 'Sharon is mustering forces, and war is coming.'

'Then,' said Prorn, 'let it come. Though the land grows cold, yet the furnaces of our armourers will stay hot enough.'

'Sire,' said the King's adviser, 'let us send a

messenger to the Elves of Taur-ea-dorpants; for if war comes, there should be alliance between our two peoples.'

But the King grew angry at this counsel. 'Elves? Never! I have sworn a great oath never again to have dealings with the Elves. Did not an elvish witch steal away my youngest son? Did not Queen Eve herself treat him as a criminal, threaten him with death, and cast him into the wilderness – where he wandered crippled in body and struck down by grief in his mind, even unto his lonely death?' For Prorn, not knowing the true fate of his son, believed this to be the truth of things. 'It was a black day for Men when Belend fell in love with that elvish sorceress, and it is better if Elf and Man keep themselves well apart.'

'But if war comes . . .'

'If Sharon invades,' roared Prorn, 'we shall meet him in battle and defeat him! We have fought him many times before, and always we have prevailed. The blood that my heart pumps is the blood of a noble line, for I am descended directly from Rokett the Man, who fought Moregothic himself in the wastelands of the north! And if the Elves trouble us, then we shall fight them too.'

And Prorn ordered granaries stocked with all available food, and instituted rations for all his people. And he also decreed that all Men with the skill to work metal should aid the armourers; and the noise of hammer chiming on anvil rang out like bells across Mannish lands. Swords were crafted, and also spears; shields were fashioned from oak and covered with tanned leather. Parchment was painted with various public messages, including *Careless Ork-Talk Costs Lives* and *Dig (in the Chest of your Enemy with a Spear) For Victory*. The land was busy with preparation for war.

In the elvish kingdoms of central Upper Middle Earth, however, the poisoning of the seasons was met with less incomprehension. For Elves, wise in the ways of nature and skilled at interpreting the flight of birds, knew that Sharon had upset the natural balance with some great spell. And they were filled with terrible foreboding.

Worse, the elvish kingdom was afflicted by the wasting away of Queen Eve. Never before had an Elf fallen sick in this manner, and Elves had previously believed that such illness was the curse only of the mortal. Yet did she sicken, and her coughing shook her like a bough troubled by the winds, and with every cough there came blood into her mouth. Eleven years she sickened. Some said that this was a punishment for having mutilated her own daughter; and some said that it was part of the malign magic that Sharon worked to turn the season back from spring to winter, but none knew how to cure her.

And after long suffering, Queen Eve died, the first Elf to die of anything other than wounds in battle. And though many thought her cruel, yet the Elves were stricken with grief.

None knew how to go on; for elfkind had always been ruled by the line of Bleary, but now the only descendant of that line of royal rank was the simulacrum of Lüthwoman. And some said, 'We must crown her Queen, for all that her head has been emptied by grief and madness'; and others said, 'She can never be queen, for she lacks all will, thought or word, and is nothing but an eidolon; and how could she reign?'

And meanwhile the two other great tribes of Elves, the Nodiholdor and the Man-Wëers, disputed amongst themselves what to do. Elsqare was one of the Nodiholdor, and he said: 'Can you not read the signs in the natural world? War is coming, and we must meet war head on. Now is not a time for internal fighting between elf and elf; but we must unite and defeat the common enemy.'

The leading Elf of the Man-Wëers was Túrin

Againdikwittingdn, and his counsel was otherwise. 'I say the Queen must be crowned, for Fate has provided us with her at this time. And if her reign is a silent one, and if she does not command us into battle, then this too is fated. Therefore, if Sharon comes, we should retreat, and let the Men confront him; go north, go west, and cede the land to him.'

'Coward!' called Elsqare in rage.

'Rather caution, which you call cowardice,' said Túrin, raging too after his fashion, 'than the reckless wildness of the Nodiholdorim, which would bring destruction upon all elfkind.'

And so a great division opened up in the heart of the elvish people. And Túrin declared that the eidolon of Lüthwoman was Queen, and readied his followers to leave that land; and Elsqare commanded his followers to prepare for war, and polish their very attractively designed armour, and make sure to clear all the dirt and grime from the lines of swirly engraving on the swords, and so on.

## Of the Breaking of the Storm

Sharon bred new Orks from the mud of Moider!, and fashioned a greater army than any had yet seen. And he pondered long how to over-ruin the whole of Upper Middle Earth, and finally he was ready.

In form he was a gigantic eyeball, so ungainly that it was quite a palaver moving him, actually; for this form was weighed down with the curse of Emu that had put him in this form. Yet he knew the Dragons' magic guaranteed him victory in battle only if he himself were present. And so he planned and pre-pared for twelve months: and this period was the first winter year, for all through its length the season remained unchanged, and frost was in the ground.

At the end of this year he used the Thing™, and his newfound Dragon power, to spawn a brood of eyeballicules. At the back of his eyeball-body was a spot to which would have been attached, had this been a regular eyeball in a regular body, the optic nerve; and with magic Sharon opened this as an orifice, and from it emerged a great stream of balls, some large as footballs, some small as insect eggs, and all sizes in between. A thousand flew out, and a thousand more, and every one was an eyeball of Sharon, through which he could see the world and influence its course. And these balls rolled about the floor in all directions, piled high. And Ork guards, running around in terror as they often did, did slip upon them, for they were roll-y under their feet as myriad marbles; and they did fall hard upon their snouts with cries of 'U-hurg!' and a clattering sound.

And the eyeball-spawn of Sharon spilled from the casements, and ran down the staircase, and many of them rolled clean away from the tower and were carried away by streams or picked up by birds. But birds that ate them could not digest them, for the Dragons' magic made Sharon invulnerable to harm, and they died and their bodies rotted where they fell.

So it was that Sharon's eyes were disseminated throughout Upper Middle Earth, and many of them remain unaccounted for even today. Many ended up being mistaken for marbles by eager marble-collecting children – a terrible mistake to make, for though they somewhat resembled marbles, and grew glassier and harder over the ages, nevertheless they were distillations of Evil; and anyone who played marbles with them would be sure to lose. Lose, I say!

With the terrible shame and despair that attends the loss of a game of marbles! Evil! Woe! Beware!

And I say to marbles-players: *you have been warned*.

This magical feat exhausted Sharon, and he slept for another twelve months. But he awoke, when eventually he did, to a new sense of the world around him, and a new power.

Sharon made his final preparations for war and conquest. Because no living horse could bear to carry Sharon, he ordered his Orks to slay ten stallions, and after death they stitched them together, and reanimated them to create a single hideous frankenstallion. And this was the terrible steed of Sharon, the big-mouthed horse of Pan-tomby – for upon this dark large-toothed steed he desired to make tombs for all, and furthermore all his constituent parts had come from the tomb, so therefore did Pan-tomby become the name of his steed. And terrible was the gnashing and chewing and swallowing that attended this steed. And if you think ordinary horse flatulence is an unpleasant thing, you should have had a whiff of what came out of this undead quadruped. And, obviously, when I say 'you should have had a whiff' I mean 'you should count yourself lucky that you never *had* a whiff'. Two words: *desolate odours*. Enough said.

Sharon took one of his eyeball-sized eyeballs, which is to say a conventional-sized eyeball, and he clothed it in a cloak, and charmed a mailed glove to hold the rein. And above his non-existent head he crowned himself with the golden crown of Supper's Ready, for he planned to devour the whole world. And he wore the Thing™ around his non-existent neck.

So Sharon the Evil rode from the tower of Cirith Connoli at the head of a mighty Army of Evil, to claim possession of all of Upper Middle Earth.

The first people of Blearyland to know of the coming of Sharon were the fishermen who dwelt on the western coast. For they fished, winter or summer, and where crops failed and fruit did not grow, Men and Elves both had traded with the fishermen. So they were doing alright, financially, thanks for asking. They got by. They were comfortable, I suppose you'd say. Actually, it's not very polite to probe into their fiscal affairs, so perhaps we'll leave that for now, if you don't mind.

One day a certain fisherman, called Wetman, was fishing in the dark mid-sea, alone in his coiled hull, when a huge-headed sea serpent rose from the waters.

'Heed me!' called this beast, and his breath came over the small ship as a stench of rotting fish, and Wetman saw the glistening roof of the monster's mouth, and its baleen teeth. He trembled, fearing that his death was come.

'Heed me!' said the serpent. 'I am Urd, and I dwell in the deeps of the ocean with my many sinuous kin. But I know this much about the dry land: the dead Men and the dead Elves of the dry land are buried in the earth, and their bodies sink slowly through the sightless ground as clods sink through water, only more slowly. And they pass eventually into underground rivers that though unseen still run, as all rivers do, to the sea. There I and my brood devour the bodies of the dead, for this is our food. Heed me! I bring fell news to the land of Men – I tell you that the age of Men and of Elves is drawing to a close. The Evil Lord has made a deal with the Dragons, and now no Elf or Man can resist him, for he is invulnerable and immortal and cannot be defeated in battle. Many will be slain in the days to come, and I say to you, and to all men, bury your dead, do not burn them in heaps. Because unless they are buried they cannot feed my brood, and if I am not fed then I shall be forced to leave the ocean and to slither across the lands in search of a meal. Heed me!'

And Wetman, shuddering with fear and cold replied, 'That's very interesting, only, um, why are you telling me this?'

And Urd said, 'Aren't you a mighty king amongst mortal Men?'

And Wetman said, 'No, I'm just a fisherman.'

And Urd said, brightly, 'Sorry! My mistake – crossed wires somewhere, I'm sure. Sorry to have bothered you.' And he sank beneath the waves.

When Wetman returned to his harbour home, dazed by this encounter and wondering how to relate it to his fellows, he discovered that the entire town was otherwise occupied. For a monstrous crowd of ocean salamanders, seawolves, marine warlocks and other horrors of the deep had come crowding out of the sea and were attacking the town. They came wet from the sea surge, and their hook-ended swords glistened, but they were strong with slimy muscle and they killed many.

The survivors fled, and made their way to the court of King Prorn, bringing their terrible tidings with them.

They were met by Men of the south, who brought terrible tidings of their own. 'Sire,' they said. 'We have dwelt for generations past on the northern bank of the mighty River Raver, and so great is its flood that none might cross it; for the river is too wide to span with a bridge, and its turbulent waters make swimming impossible, and it is treacherous for boats. And for an age Orks have sometimes crossed in little boats, and we have sometimes fought with them, but only a few at a time can cross by this route. But now a dire fate has befallen us.'

And the King did ask, 'What?'

'The River has frozen solid as far west as the Bend of E,' said the Men of the south. 'For we have had nothing but winter for twenty-four months, without spring or summer to thaw the chill. And now a mighty host of Orks has crossed the ice, and has driven all Men and Elves from the southlands. None have been able to stand against them.'

At this terrible news, the cry of 'Sorrow!' was taken up in the streets of Mantown, and people left their houses and came into the open. 'Should we fly?' they said. 'Gather our belongings and move north?'

'No!' said the King, standing in his stirrups to address the crowd in the main square, 'we must not flee, or we will be forever on the run. We shall meet this army of Orks and defeat it in battle!' And some of his people slipped away to the north with their most precious things in sacks on their backs, for a dread was in their hearts; and others ignored their despair and strapped on their armour.

News of the advancing army of Orks reached Elfton as well; where the Coward Elves, as they were called, had long been making their preparations for departure. 'The time has come,' they said. 'Why die in pointless battle? By flight we remain immortal.'

And Elsqare and his elves replied, 'Take your blank Queen and leave if you will. But is there anywhere to flee? It seems to me that you do nothing but postpone the inevitable end of all things.'

And Túrin replied, 'Must you *always* be so gloomy? Would it *kill* you to think positively just once?'

To which Elsqare said, 'I'm only saying . . .'

And Túrin continued, 'You're a real mug-of-mead-half-empty sort of elf, aren't you?'

And Elsqare, rather wounded in his feelings, said stiffly, 'I like to think of myself as a realist.'

'Pessimist, rather,' said Túrin.

'At least I'm not a coward,' snapped Elsqare.

'Oh, you're *wild*,' said Túrin, perhaps speaking ironically, it's not obvious, but certainly not meaning anything praiseworthy by the word. And Túrin left with his followers and they made their way west. But they encountered a marauding band of sea-monsters and Orks, and doubled back on themselves, trekking across the northern grassplains to Lothlomondwisky.

The last army of Men, and the last army of Elves, marched out to meet the horde of Orks on the Plain of Crossed Swords. And there they arrayed themselves, on separate sides of the battlefield. And neither army would so much as talk with the other, because each side blamed the other for the whole Belend and Lüthwoman thing. The Men viewed Lüthwoman as 'no better than she ought to be', which phrase the Elves did not quite understand but which they assumed was meant to be insulting. On their side, however, the Elves viewed Belend as a gigolo, a lounger, a chancer, and a seducer who had had his wicked way with the pure daughter of Queen Eve.

The Men did say 'Your elvish seductress brought about tragedy and the death of the King's son.'

The Elves did say 'Well if it comes to that – your priapic young man brought about the madness of the Queen's daughter *and* the death of the Queen *and* the ending of the royal line Bleary which stretched to the beginning of time, which trumps your distress I think. Besides, though the King's son died – well, he was a mortal Man and doomed to die sooner or later.

But Queen Eve was an immortal Elf, and did not deserve her fate.'

The Men did consider this argument, and after much thought did reply, 'Yah!'. And some of them did display their naked hindquarters to the elvish soldiers, who looked away with expressions of haughty disgust.

And so there was no prospect of alliance between the armies, even though they faced the same enemy.

And so it was that the army of Sharon swarmed over the horizon. It was the largest gathering of Orks ever seen under the skies of Upper Middle Earth. It stretched the whole of the horizon from east to west, and its troops poured on and on as if fed by a ceaseless source. Some Orks were albino-white and foul to see, and some were green-skinned and icky, and they had noses, some more than one. But many had only one functioning eye, having torn out the other in honour of Sharon their leader whom they honoured as a god, even though this resulted in them having greatly lessened depth-perception capacities. And they were armoured with heavy iron breast-plates, and wore Le Creuset helmets of great weight and solidity.

Soon they covered the whole ground with their

number, and they chanted in terrible unison 'Blood! Blood! Blood!' and stamped their iron-shod feet in time, and the tremors travelled through the ground to the armies of Elves and Men.

And then they fell silent, for they sensed the arrival of their Lord and Leader was near. And the silence was more terrible to the Men and Elves than the chanting.

Prorn the King called across the space to the Elvish army, saying 'You're always ready with a wise-crack, Elsqare, say something to lighten the mood.'

Elsqare looked out at the thick crush of orkish bodies, and said only, 'Actually, nothing very comical occurs to me.'

So Prorn turned to his own men and called out, 'Be ready to fight, and be not afraid to die, if die you must. But fight!' And his men cheered, although it sounded but a weakly hurrah in the cold air.

And Elsqare turned to his men, and said in a clear bell-like voice: 'Unaccustomed as I am to pre-battle speeches, I would just like to take a moment to thank you all for turning up, many of you at terribly short notice. Believe me it's *very* much appreciated. And I'd like to thank the caterers for supplying the salted meats – it may be two years old, but it tastes no more than fourteen months.'

And a smattering of applause rippled through the elvish army.

As one the Orks began calling 'Doom! Doom!', and this created a deep rumbling wash of sound. For Sharon was approaching on his horse Pan-tomby. A path cleared through the horizon-spanning tangled thicket of orkish warriors, and Sharon rode forward.

And at the sight of him all hope left the hearts of the Men and the Elves; for the Dragons' charm made Sharon their master, and their wills were not enough to fight the potency of this magic. The irony of the spell was that the truest warriors, whose loyalty was strongest, were least able to fight – because their hearts told them that Sharon was their true and liege lord; whilst at the same time the most fickle of the soldiers, whose sense of loyalty was weakest, were best motivated to defend themselves, for they barely recognised any master but themselves in the first place.

Many threw their weapons and themselves on the ground in despair; and Prorn himself wavered. 'Blearyland,' he called to the high heavens. 'A cursed land, named for a cursed king. And so the curse works itself out in blood and death.'

And the Orks laughed and jeered, and some coughed and cheered, and some others acted daft and weird, and others otherwise expressed their delight in their imminent and total victory.

Sharon pulled up his terrible frankenstallion at the head of his army, and rose up in his stirrups. And, with the power of the Thing™ he cast his voice into the sky so that every elvish and every mannish soldier could hear it.

'Hearken!' he called. And because his voice was projected at a point close to the Thing™ itself, there was a shrieky feedbacky sort of noise that made Orks, Men and Elves alike duck their heads down and clutch their ears and wince markedly. So Sharon made certain adjustments.

'Sorry about that,' he said. 'That's better. So – hearken! Listen to me, you the last army of Elves, and you the last army of Men. Know this, that the Dragons of Making have granted me a fourfold charm: and that by their magic I am lord over all Men and all Elves forever – and that I am invulnerable, and immortal, and invincible in battle. Purge your hearts of hope! Your doom is to die, or else live on as my slaves.'

And Sharon laughed, and his laughter was thunder in the mountains, and the rattling of the wings of innumerable crows ascending in winter skies, and the grumbling of icebergs. He went: 'Ha ha ha ha ha!

Ah-*ha* ha ha! Ah-ho ho ho! Ah-ha-ha ha! Ah-ha-ha
ha!' And, furthermore he went: 'Ha! Ha! Ha! Ha!
Ha! Ha! Ha! Ha! Ha! Ha! Ha! Ha! Ha! Ha! Ha!
Ha! Ha! Ha! Ha! Ha! Ha! Ha! Ha! Ha! Ha! Ha!
Ha! Ha! Ha! HA! HA! HA! HA! HA! HA! HA!
HA! HA! HA! HA! HA! HA! HA! HA! **HA!
HA! HA! HA! HA! HA! HA! HA! HA!
HA! HA! HA! HA! HA! HA!**' And he laughed so
hard he made himself wheezy, and had to sit back
down in the saddle, saying 'Oh, dear, oh dear, oh.
Dear.'

And the Orks cheered.

But the last hope perished in the breasts of Men
and Elves, for they knew in their hearts that what
Sharon said was true: every Elf and every Man was
drawn to Sharon as lord. Some fled, deserting their
comrades in this darkest hour; some ran towards the
orkish army with their arms up; and only a very few
remained about their leaders.

And Sharon called, 'Charge!'

And so his myriad Orks bellowed and howled
with blood lust, and surged forward, like floodwaters
made flesh and armed with steel. They cut down
those few Men and Elves who had run forward to
declare their allegiance to Sharon, for they were
careless of whom they killed.

The two armies of Men and Elves that remained were nothing but rumps; yet, through sheer blind habit, or else through some twist of character that resisted the Dragons' charms, they readied themselves for the fight. Prorn himself raised his sword and screamed, a scream such as a wind-spirit[24] might make in the height of the tempest; and in this sound he found release from the agony of conflicted loyalties the appearance of Sharon had produced in his breast. And he stepped forward as the front rank of slathering Orks crashed upon him; and he swung his sword from left to right, cutting down three enemy warriors, and he swung his sword from right to left and cut down two more, and then the crush overwhelmed him. And his body was slashed by many hatchets and trampled under many iron-shod feet, and the life was cut and crushed from his frame. And so ended the life of King Prorn III, known as the Grrreat.

His bodyguard fought as well as they could, though hopelessly outnumbered. And for a little while the very size of the Ork army prevented them from making their victory an immediate thing, for

---

24 A zephyr, or Spirit of the Howling Gale; not a clockwork spirit of the sort that keeps your wristwatch wound over a period of several years.

the Men stood in a circle with their weapons out, and only a certain number of Orks could present themselves at any one assault. So the Men fought on, cutting and hacking, until a wall of ork corpses grew before them; yet Orks still clambered over the top of this and rained down blows and axe-ended spears upon them. One by one the guard of Men perished. Prince Stronginthearm, Prorn's strong-armed first-born, died of a gash that cut his head in twain.[25] Prince Braveface, Prorn's second-born, died under a savage barrage of hook-ended swords.

Nor did the Elves do better. They fought with elegant coordination, sweeping their long gold-decorated steel lances to and fro and clearing great swathes from the mass of advancing Orks. But there were always more Orks to come clambering over the bodies of their fallen, and soon even the strength of the Elves was exhausted, and their formation was overrun. Some Elves died there and then; some were carried off to be mutilated or torn to pieces by howling bands of Orks; and some few were captured by Sharon's personal bodyguard – who alone of the horde possessed a modicum of self-restraint amongst all the blood lust and berserker fury and such.

---

25  Which is to say, into twelve pieces.

And so Sharon had brought before him a dozen
Elves and fewer Men, clad about with cruel iron-
thorned chains, their hands bound at their backs.
And they were forced to kneel before the Evil One
and his terrible steed on the blood-sodden ground.

'Yield,' he called, 'and swear allegiance to me as
your Lord, and I shall not kill you quite yet. For I
have need of slaves, and my torments may yet spare
you for years yet.'

With the Dragons' magic pressing upon their
heart neither elf nor man could resist. Elsqare the
Elf, the last Nodiholdor of noble blood still alive,
swore allegiance to Sharon the Dark Lord. And so
did all the Elves, and all the Men.

So ended the last battle, with evil victorious. The
Orks of Sharon's horde spent their fury, making the
land around the battlefield a wasteland in their berserker rage, until the rage passed off them and they
had a berserker hangover. Which only made them
grumpier. And there really wasn't enough berserker-
seltzer in the stores of the medical orderlies to go
round, and some people got very snappish and
unhappy, let me tell you.

And Sharon rode to Elfton, with his captives in
chains behind him, and made it his new capital. Thus

came to an end the history of Men and Elves; for neither lived happily ever after – the Men, because they were mortal and could not live ever after, regardless of their mood; and the Elves, because although they *could* live ever after, it was very hard for them to be happy under the new regime.

Sharon rode about his new kingdom, and in every place he came he commanded automatic fealty, because the Dragons' magic was strong. And even if elf or man had been able to stand against him, they would have faced the fundamental problem of his invulnerability, immortality and invincibility. Which is, I hope you agree, something of a poser.

# Of the Tyranny of Sharon, or the 'Sharonny' as it was called

Sharon exulted in his victory. He established a capital for his new empire on the site of Elfton. 'Pull down this elf town,' he ordered the Elves of Taur-ea-dorpants. 'You shall build me a new capital.' And the inhabitants of Elfton were compelled by their malign allegiance to tear apart their own homes and temples, and scatter the debris.

And Sharon set ork overseers over gangs of Men and Elves, to quarry and drag great stones, to cut timber with giant scythes and fashion it, and to build up a vast new building. He commanded men to sieve the lakes of Blearyland for gems to decorate his throne; and to lay down hundreds of fleeces to pan gold from the flowing streams; and ordered Elves to labour twenty hours in the day to raise up the great blocks of stone.

And so, over twelve months of the hardest labour, and many deaths, a great and stark palace uprose. And largely it was composed of rectangles and blocks, and these were built in an uparching lopsided dome, tall as a mountain. And inside was a huge green-black hall, and here Sharon's great lidless eye sat in state upon a vast eggcup of gold, for this, he had discovered, was the best shape for his throne. And all the leaders of Men and Elves left alive trooped into this hall, before the sneering and mockery of phalanxes of Orks, and paid homage to Sharon.

His new capital he called The Sharonage, and over the gateway he placed a sign that read: *Dunberserkin*.

Sharon sent out Tuoni Bleary and Robin Badfellow to scout the land for twenty strong, tall individuals, ten elvish and ten mannish, and these were brought bound to the Sharonage, although they were not tortured or broken. For Sharon required their bodies to be strong.

And they were bound to metal frames in one of the dungeons of the new fortress, and ork surgeons clustered around them, grunting and chuckling; and into the chambers rolled and bounced two score of Sharon's brood of eyeballs, swarming over the black flagstones like hideous insects, rolling and squeaking.

And each of these Men and each of the Elves had their own eyes pulled out with bill-ended tongs; and into the oozing sockets the ork servants pushed two of Sharon's eyeball offspring. Yuk. I mean, I'm sorry

to have to relate that last bit, which is pretty repuls-
ive I know, but, you know. The story requires it. So
if you've stopped shuddering, we can proceed.

And when this foul surgery was completed the
Men and Elves were released from their frames to
fall to the floor in despair. And some of them burned
in their hearts to end their lives at that time, and
some burned to seize metal pokers or blades and kill
as many as they could. But all were bound by the
Dragons' curse, that Sharon be lord over all Elves
and Men, for as long as Elves and Men exist. And
Sharon commanded them to take horse and ride
about Blearyland making his will known to Elves
and Men, and to give him – as he sat in the Sharonage – views of the land he now ruled.

These twenty individuals were called the Eyes
of Sharon, although they were known to Men and
Elves as the Scary Score of Scanners: and their
tragedy was that they served Sharon's evil through
no fault of their own, for they were noble spirits, but
of a fell necessity. And though they were compelled
to do as Sharon commanded them, yet did all Men
and Elves shun the Scary Score. They fed them, and
gave them shelter, and surrendered their horses to
them, because they must; but they loathed them all
the same.

And Sharon set his most trusty subalterns as lords over the various shires and provinces of Blearyland, and laid a heavy tax upon them but gave them free rein to treat their underlings as they wished. And for those of the Orks who craved manflesh or elf-flesh to eat, they were permitted to purchase this food for a certain price. And for those who yearned to command troops of mannish slaves, or to force Elves to labour in the fields, they were permitted to do this.

Many copses were burnt; and many creatures killed; for winter continued to prevail in the land, and the myriad Orks were hungry. So many trees were burnt to heat the soil, and many forest animals were slain and eaten.

And yet did Sharon grow uneasy even in his triumph, for he thought again and again of the Dragons' magic. And whilst he could see no weakness in the promise of invulnerability, immortality or invincibility, yet he pondered the fact that he had been granted dominion over only Elves and Men. He thought of the creatures of Upper Middle Earth that were neither elvish nor mannish, and worried over the harm they might do him.

So he sent some of his Eyes to treat with the Dwarfs; but they were uninterested in the happenings in the lands of Men and Elves, being mostly concerned with their own subterranean affairs. 'Leave us alone, bach,' they said, 'and we'll leave you alone. Common sense, that.'

Yet still Sharon fretted. So he sent a command through the whole kingdom, that any person who knew of any danger to his might from a being outside the realm of Men and Elves, should declare it. And none could resist this command.

One day a man approached the gateway of the Sharonage. The fir-needles were tooth-white with frost, and the crust of ice on the snow cracked under his feet leaving deep pitted footprints, and the sky was blue with perfect cold.

And he begged entrance, to approach Sharon himself. 'Why?' demanded the gate-guard in scorn. 'In answer to his command,' replied the man, with great grief in his voice.

He was led to the throne-hall, and Sharon's great lidless eyeball did stare down upon him. 'Why have you come?' he asked.

'In answer to your command, O Lord,' said the man.

'Speak!' said Sharon eagerly. 'Tell me!'

And the man said, 'I was a fisherman, and one day at sea I encountered a sea creature called Urd, who told me that he and his brood in the deep waters feed upon the bodies of dead Men and Elves, buried in the earth, that wash out eventually to the ocean. He warned me that should we stop burying our dead in the earth, then he and his brood would go hungry, and would leave the ocean and swarm over the land to eat.'

Sharon was glad to learn of this, for Urd was such a creature as was not covered in the Dragons' charm; and though he knew himself still invulnerable, immortal and invincible, yet he had no wish to encounter this sea serpent.

As he told his tale, the fisherman wept. And Sharon asked, 'Why do you weep?'

And the fisherman was compelled by the charm to answer him truly. 'I weep to have revealed this to you, my lord. For although I and my kind are all prevented from rebelling against you, yet I yearned to see this realm of yours wasted by these sea beasts, for my heart is dead with bitterness at your dominion.'

Sharon laughed at this. 'Truly!' he said. 'Well, fisherman, *my* desire is to increase your woe. So we must appease these Sea Beasts. You shall ride out with these half dozen of my Eyes, to the lands of the west that abut the sea. And there you yourself shall choose fifty people from each village and a hundred from each town; and they shall be slain by my Orks and buried in the ground, as offerings to Urd. I command you to do this thing, and then to return here to me to see what other tasks I may have for you.'

The fisherman wept at this, and yet had no choice but to obey. And in this barbarous manner was the threat of Urd abated by Sharon.

And Sharon sent his Eyes throughout the land, and ordered all Elves and Men to swear an oath that they would never plot against him, seek to overthrow him, or rise up. And with tears and despair, all swore this oath. For they could not do otherwise.

## *Of Eärwiggi*

Once there was a boy called Eärwiggi, which in Elvish means 'ceremonial earmuff made of horsehair'; and in after times he was sometimes called Eärwiggi of the Mighty Fib, for his destiny was bound up with a fib that could bring down evil empires and change the very fabric of the world. It is a strange and instructive story, and its moral is: always tell the truth – unless telling a *small* fib can bring down evil empires and change the very fabric of the world.

Now Eärwiggi was born in a small home on the banks of the River Optik, and he grew up there with his mother and father. He grew strong and tall, and learnt how to fish from the river, and how to take the honey from bees without being stung by them; and he learnt which forest fruit and mushroom are good to eat, and which not.

He had neither brother nor sister, and there were no neighbours nearby; but from time to time visitors would come by, to trade with his parents, or travelling to some other place and hoping for refreshment; and some of these visitors were elven, and some were

Men, but never Elves and Men at the same time. And when he asked his parents about this they said: 'Once in this land Elves and Men were friends; but there has been a falling out recently, and now no Elf and no Man will greet the other in friendship.'

'What sort of falling out?' asked Eärwiggi, for he was always curious.

But his parents were reticent. 'Oh,' they said. 'Grown-up stuff.' And they taught him the stories and traditions of both Men and Elves.

And then one year there came dire news from the outside world. It was said that the land languished under winter when it should be spring. But although the rest of Blearyland was laid over by winter, yet the field and hollow by Eärwiggi's home, and the bank of the river there, were not afflicted. Visitors were amazed to discover this; the only place in the world not afflicted by the curse of ice.

'Something terrible is abroad,' said one broad-bearded man who had come to trade metal for smoked fish, and fabrics woven by Eärwiggi's mother. The trade had been made, and now he sat in their hearth drinking ale. 'Some say that Sharon has made a pact with the Dragons of Making, a terrible spell. They say that he will cast the world in an endless winter.'

Eärwiggi was sitting under the table, holding its leg, as he sometimes did. And he could see his parents exchange a mysterious look between them.

The trader noticed it too, by the firelight. 'Yet you are free of the curse here,' he said. 'The land outside your walls is fresh with late spring, when the rest of Blearyland is frozen and dead. How can this be?'

'We do not know,' said Eärwiggi's father.

The trader stared hard at both of them. When he spoke eventually, it was with a grim tone: 'Some say that you are enchanters. Is it so?'

Eärwiggi's father shook his head sorrowfully in the firelight.

But the trader would not stay. Though it was dark outside, and bitterly cold beyond the borders of this house, yet he gathered his things and left. After that very few traders came, and soon Eärwiggi was left with none but his parents for company.

Eärwiggi reached the age of eleven, which is an important age of transition to the elvish people, the age they say when a boy ceases to be a child. And on this day Eärwiggi's father took him to the copse by the river to teach him the arts of boat-building. And they worked at this in the day, although it was no labour for Eärwiggi delighted in it and accounted it play. And they worked again the following day, and the day after.

As they worked together, Eärwiggi said to his father: 'Father, I am worried.'

'Worried about what, my son?'

'It seems to me that I am akin to the travellers who come here, and not akin to you and mother.'

'Aching?' asked his father.

'Akin,' clarified Eärwiggi.

His father laughed aloud at such a strange statement by his son, and said, 'Why would you say so?'

'The travellers who come here have two hands, as do I. Yet you and mother have each but one hand. Are you a different race to the Elves and the Men of whom you have told me?'

His father shook his head, and wiped sweat from his beard with the crook of his arm. 'No, son,' he said. 'I lost my hand to a wild beast, and your mother lost hers to – an accident. Together they are only a pair of accidental injuries. But you are our son, created by the two of us together.' And he drew his son to him and hugged him.

That afternoon, after the boat-building was done, Eärwiggi knew his last purely happy day. And in later years he thought back to this day, and thought that there must be such a moment in all lives; a transition point from the carelessness of childhood to the anxieties of the fully grown. Such a moment can only be known afterwards, when time has already swallowed it; but it remains sweet for all that.

The moment was by the river. The landscape in the distance was austere; the mountains in the east cold and tall, and even the hills to the south were capped with snow. Yet the land around Eärwiggi's home was green. He stood knee-deep in the grass watching the river flow smoothly past; and the surface of the river was touched by motes like stars in a moving sky as water boatmen stood upon the water. Fruit trees that grew behind the house were feathery with blossom. A cicada hidden somewhere in the grass tried its voice by fits, as if practising upon a long unused instrument.

He heard shouting from the front of the house, and the moment broke.

Running round to the front he found his father and mother standing in their doorway, and a band of men on horseback in the road before them. The leader was the spade-bearded trader who had sometimes visited. 'Sharon has walked an army across the frozen River Raver into Blearyland,' he called, and his face was red with choler. 'The King has ordered all Men to join the army, for we must fight the last great battle now.'

Eärwiggi's father said nothing, but it was clear from his face that he did not intend to go with these people.

'Are you not a Man?' bellowed the trader, leaning down and shaking a sword in his wrath. 'Can you deny it?'

This puzzled Eärwiggi, for he had thought his father elven, and had assumed that he himself was elven also. But his father did not deny that he was a Man, only folded his arms across his chest.

'Why would you not fight?' growled the trader, 'a man with a family in the face of such a threat? Are you a coward? Or – are you in truth a sorcerer? Have you made some deal with Sharon?'

'No!' said Eärwiggi's father, fiercely.

And the horses of the band of Men started and shuffled their hooves. And the trader leant back in his saddle; until one of the other Men said, 'Kevin, he's crippled, a one-handed man – maybe that's why he's loath to fight.'

And the trader glowered, and said nothing. And then the Men wheeled their horses and rode away, except for one man whose horse farted as he spurred it, and danced up on its hind legs tossing him to the floor.

And it was peaceful in Eärwiggi's home once more.

Week followed week, and Eärwiggi heard no further tidings of the world outside. Yet he wondered about the great battle being fought to the south; and he tried to imagine the clash of weapons, the stern charges of soldiery, the bravery and the dying. But one morning Eärwiggi got up from his bed to find his parents sitting downstairs simply staring at one another.

'What's wrong?' he asked.

'Eärwiggi,' said his father. 'A dark hand has touched our hearts. Some dreadful thing has happened in this land, and it has touched our spirits. We fear the worst. If anything should happen to us, you must travel far from here: to the north and the west, on the northern bank of the river, and far away. Do you understand?'

Eärwiggi said he understood, although his heart was unready.

The weeks continued to pass, and Eärwiggi and his parents went about their usual business, but something had changed. His father and mother were spirit-broken, oppressed by some heaviness within their hearts that saddened Eärwiggi even though he could not understand it. And though they had no tidings, yet they knew that the battle had gone badly for Mankind.

And one day a band of Orks appeared and at their head a strange shrunken figure, with something of an elvish cast to his features and yet without the dignity or beauty of an elf. His large lips wriggled like slippery ropes, alternately revealing and concealing a set of teeth that a good-sized goat would have been proud to own. Inverted J eyebrows of exaggerated size gave a supercilious cast to his protuberantly gobstopper eyes. He was wearing motley like a jester, but motley full of holes and covered in many splattery stains. It was, in fact, mottled and mothy motley.

'I am Bleary,' he announced, 'and I am your new King, or more strictly your sub-king, a sort of junior king or kingling, serving the community here under the overlordship of Sharon. Who is Big King. I heard in the town upriver that a patch of ground here is still in spring, when the rest of Sharonia is in winter, and I see that it is true. Can you explain it?'

'We cannot,' said Eärwiggi's father.

'Hmm,' said Bleary. 'Hum. Most odd. Ah well, I

like it here. I shall make this my official country residence. You,' (he pointed at Eärwiggi's father) 'and you' (he pointed at Eärwiggi's mother) 'are commanded by Sharon himself to make your way to the place formerly known as Elfton, to help with municipal construction.'

Eärwiggi's father stepped forward at this command, and Eärwiggi clutched his leg, saying 'Father, do not obey this command!'

And his father replied, in a low voice. 'I cannot help myself. Run, son. Flee this place. Do not go south, for that way will lead you to Sharon and your doom. Go north, and west, and find if there be any free place left in Blearyland.'

And he walked through the door, and his wife walked with him, helpless against the command; and they walked without resting until they reached Elfton, and a dark fate.

But Bleary, looking over his new property, and shooing away Orks who were chasing chickens across the yard, came upon Eärwiggi sitting underneath the table in the hearth room. 'What's this?' he said. 'Sprog, is it? Thinking back, I did specify the man and the woman with my command. This damn Dragon magic – you've got to be so careful to phrase these things precisely, or objects fall through the net.

Alright, you little tyke. I am *ordering* you, on behalf of Sharon the mighty, to follow your parents – walk south, do not stop until you reach Elfton, and join in the construction work. Off you go.'

So confident was Bleary of the power of the command that the Dragons' magic gave him, in the name of Sharon, that he paid no more attention to the boy; and his Orks were gorging themselves on the homestead's livestock in the barn, and he hurried out to remonstrate with them. So Eärwiggi hurried from the house.

But he did not walk south. Instead he crept down to the river, and the boat that he had built with his father, and he pushed this into the water and climbed in, lying down in the bottom of it, and allowing the waters to carry him west.

Eärwiggi's boat took him down the long stretches of the River Optik and into the broad amber waters of the Lothlomondwisky. He paddled the boat to the northern shore, and pulled it into the sand. Using a fallen bough he levered it over to make a roof, and burrowed under the sand at the stern to make an entrance. With thread and hook, and a twist of his hair as lure, he caught a salmon in the stream, and cooked it on a driftwood fire.

But the land here was barren with snow, and Eärwiggi underneath his boat-roof slept poorly because of the cold. He was still tired when the morning came, and he rubbed his eyes and pondered his fate as he walked beside the lake. The shore of the lake was sandy, with pebbles set in the sand. And when he looked more closely at the sand he saw that it was composed of tiny fragments of thin shells, broken by waves into patterns of miniature crescents and stars and other shapes, shells frail as paper. He thought to himself: did shrimp and watersnails think their shells would keep them safe in such a world?

Now, the winter was severe across Blearyland, but more severe still further north; and the wolves of the far north had been driven south by weather extreme even for them. They flocked from the Wa!-Wastes into Illbhavior, and roamed the northern shores of the River Optik. And as Eärwiggi wandered lone and lorn, a pack of wolves scented him. And they came in a tight pack, loping across the sand.

Eärwiggi saw them approach, and thought quickly. He looked to the frost-furred trees at the top of the beach, and looked to the swiftly approaching pack of wolves. And he ran, fast as his eleven-year-old legs could run: but not to the trees. Instead he ran straight into the amber waters of the lake, and swam out. The water was cold as death is cold, and Eärwiggi gasped; but still he swam.

The wolves gathered on the water's margin, but did not come any closer. They turned and turned in tight circles, with their long shaggy muzzles and yellow eyes always pointing at Eärwiggi, waiting for the time when he was too tired and was forced to come ashore. For a while Eärwiggi trod water, and wondered what to do.

But then he heard somebody speaking a language he did not understand; and the words of this language were as follows: 'Bach! glub! glub! over*yeer*! Look you!'

And looking around Eärwiggi saw a figure floundering in the water, a little way from where he was. So he swam over to the figure, crying aloud with the cold as he pushed his arms through the water.

'Hello,' said the figure. His broad head was just visible above the water, but Eärwiggi was aware of the furious action of his limbs underneath the surface.

'Hello,' said Eärwiggi.

'Bit of bother, look you,' said the figure. 'A little help would be very special.'

'Alright,' said Eärwiggi. 'What's the problem?'

'The problem is that my beard, like, is tied to a boulder under the water. On the lake bed, do you see, blub-glub.'

'How did that happen?'

'Oh, it's a long story, actually. But, you see, what with the beard tying me here I've been treading water. For quite a long time in fact. We Dwarfs we're strong, and good on endurance, but there's a limit, and I'm not far off that limit now, I'd say.'

'Oh dear.'

'If you'd be so good as to swim down – you can feel your way down the beard like a hairy anchor chain. Unsnag it, and I'll be forever in your debt.'

So Eärwiggi took a deep breath, and dived under the water. It was many yards to the lakebed, and he pulled himself down the dwarf's beard through the peat-red waters. He could see his way as he swam, but he felt down to a slimy smooth boulder, around which the dwarf's beard had been wrapped and tied. Though the water was cold enough to chill his heart-beat, and though he worked blind, yet Eärwiggi had nimble fingers and he was soon able to unpick the knot.

He struggled to the surface, and took as deep a breath as his frozen lungs allowed him. 'I can't thank you enough,' said the Dwarf. 'I was on the verge of going under the water then, I don't mind telling you. Let's get over to the shore.'

'There are,' Eärwiggi panted, 'wolves . . .'

'Bah,' said the Dwarf. 'Wolves? Neither year nor there.'

'Year?' said Eärwiggi, who was confused and weary with the great cold.

'Come on,' said the Dwarf. He splashed over to the beach with strokes of his little arms. And the wolves saw him coming, and gathered in a pack. The Dwarf reached the shore as the wolves prepared to lunge for him, each animal competing with its fellow for first bite. But the Dwarf plucked heavy pebbles from the sand under the shallow water, and hurled them with his muscular arms. A first pebble struck the lead wolf between its eyes and split its skull; a second caught another wolf in the same spot, with the same result. The Dwarf drew back his arm for a third throw, and the remaining wolves turned their tails and ran for the treeline.

The Dwarf collapsed face down in the water. As Eärwiggi dragged him up the beach, with no small effort, and many fallings-over, he murmured, 'Glad that second stone sent the rest away. I wouldn't have had the strength for a third throw, look you. That's what three days and three nights treading water will do for your muscles, la.'

Eärwiggi dragged the Dwarf to the upturned boat, and left him under cover there. Then he caught more fish from the stream, and lit a fire, and dried himself and his clothes, and did the same for the Dwarf's clothes. And after sleeping for many hours, and eating his fill of fish, and wringing out his beard and plaiting it and tying it several times around his waist, the Dwarf became more much conversational.

'My name,' he said, 'is Nobbi. And I am in your debt, young fellow.'

'My name is Eärwiggi. And I am in yours. Debt I mean. For you drove off the wolves.'

'Driving off wolves? That's sport, that is. Don't mention it.'

'Sir Nobbi,' said Eärwiggi, 'where are you from? For I notice that you say *thass* instead of that's, and *year* instead of here.'

'Dwarfish accent, that,' said Nobbi. 'Mel. Oh. Dios. *I* think so, any rate.'

'And how did you come to be tied to the rock at the bed of the lake?'

'Ah,' said the Dwarf. 'Long story.'

'We have time.'

'Not for this story. No, when I say long, I mean long. *Long*. Last all winter in the telling.'

'They say the winter will never end.'

'Well,' said the Dwarf. 'Quite. What about you?'

'My parents have been made into slaves by the Evil One, Sharon. He has overrun the whole of Blearyland, and made all the people into slaves; for a Dragon's spell has given him dominion over all Men and Elves for as long as there are men and elves.'

'Hmm,' grunted Nobbi, in assent. 'Politics, is it?'

'Politics?'

'Always *some* politics going on with Men and Elves and Orks. Good one season, evil the next. The way I see it, good, evil, whichever: the government always gets in.'

'I don't understand,' said Eärwiggi.

'If I was you, boy,' the Dwarf continued, 'I'd take a dwarfish perspective on things. I mean, if fighting the ultimate battle of good against evil actually *changed* anything, they'd make it illegal. Don't you think?'

Eärwiggi pondered this. 'You do sound a little disillusioned with the whole political system, Sir Nobbi.'

'Disillusioned?' said the Dwarf. 'Perhaps I am a

little jaded, la, with the two-party system. Why does it have to be *either* good *or* evil, see? Why can't we have a ethical system that truly represents the rainbow of moral positions real people adopt in the real world, see?'

But this conversation was only puzzling to Eärwiggi's head. 'Surely I should be good – shouldn't I? Strive at all times to tell the truth, for instance?'

'Truth,' said Nobbi, knowingly.

'Isn't the truth better than lies?'

'Sometimes,' said the Dwarf, tapping his prodigious nose.

'At any rate,' said Eärwiggi, 'I still hope for the final victory of good over evil.'

'You think?' said the Dwarf. 'Why?'

'Well,' said Eärwiggi. 'My parents told me many stories as I grew up about the history of Upper Middle Earth, and in all of them it seemed that good was defeated, that catastrophe was inevitable, that evil was about to prevail for all time – until at the *very last minute*, with the last glimmer of hope, good triumphed.'

'Stories,' said Nobbi, sucking the last flesh from the bones of the salmon Eärwiggi had caught. 'You think because it's been like that in history so far, that it'll be like that in the future? Why should it?' He flourished his hand in the air with a turning motion, and said, 'Good triumphs at the last against the odds one time. Good triumphs at the last against the odds a second time. Good triumphs at the last against the odds a third time, la. Does it seem likely to you that it's going to go on and on like that?'

'Um,' said Eärwiggi. He could feel the last ember of hope dying in his heart, and it was an uncomfortable feeling, a bit like indigestion but more spiritual.

'Pooh,' said Nobbi, by which he meant to express dismissive scorn. 'If you toss a coin and it comes up 'eads six times in a row, do you say to yourself "well this *proves* that no matter how many times I toss this coin, it'll always turns up 'eads?" Is *that* your logic?'

'So you're saying . . .'

'Law of averages, isn't it,' said the Dwarf. 'Sooner or later evil is bound to triumph. *That's* politics, see.'

'So Sharon is now Lord of Upper Middle Earth for ever?'

'Could be.'

'And has evil finally triumphed after all? It is a grim thought.'

'What was it you said the Dragon magic said? For as long as there are Elves and Men? Best get used to it.'

'But if I fall into the hands of the Orks, they'll

make me a slave and work me to death – or eat me – or otherwise crush my spirit and destroy me.'

'Master Eärwiggi, you saved me from drowning, and you've fed me, and I'll repay you by keeping you out of the 'ands of the Orks. Where are you travelling?'

'West,' said Eärwiggi, remembering his parents' words. 'And north.'

'Cold up north,' said Nobbi. 'But I've always wanted to go west. So west we'll go.'

And the first thing Nobbi did was to draw forth a myth-army knife from his belt, and with it to skin the two wolf carcasses.

'You mean,' said Eärwiggi, 'that you had that knife all along? Why didn't you just cut your beard with it and swim free?'

'Cut my beard, bach?' said Nobbi, horrified. 'Do you *hear* what you're saying? Cut my own beard? That's sacrilege, that is.'

And he scraped the skins and dried them in the wind; and he cooked the meat and salted it at a salt-lick nearby; and when the skins were ready he wrapped himself in one and Eärwiggi in the other.

In this fashion, protected against the winter and with a small store of food, the Dwarf and the boy travelled together, moving west along the northern shoreline of the Loth. And they had many adventures, too many to relate here, frankly.

They passed through a desolate landscape, white as summer clouds but chill as death; and the northern wind was a malicious thing, that insinuated itself in at the crevices and rents in their garments and seemed to cut their skin with its very chill.

At last they reached the western seaboard.

They found a camp of two dozen Elves, who were sitting on the strand in a state of considerable dejection. The shell of a boat, half-built, was abandoned on the shore behind them. The Elves sat before their tents, staring at the sea with eyes full of misery.

When Eärwiggi and Nobbi came upon them they were, at first, full of terror thinking them Orks come to kill; and when they saw that the newcomers were not Orks, they fell to tears and wailing. Eärwiggi had never seen Elves crying before.

But this was not the most amazing thing to Eärwiggi; for as he looked around the group he thought he saw his mother, sitting on a rock and looking out at the ocean with a blank face. He approached her and cried out 'Mother!' And though she looked at his face, there was no recognition in her expression.

'Wait,' said the Elves, running over, 'what are you doing?'

'This is my mother,' said Eärwiggi, his eyes full of tears, 'although she pretends not to recognise me.'

'Your mother?' cried the elves. 'Never! This is our Queen, and she has never taken to herself a husband, or borne children. For, as we think, the evil of Sharon has stolen her wits, and left her mind smooth and blank as a new fall of snow over the fields. She cannot be your mother.'

Yet, through his tear-blurred eyes, it seemed to Eärwiggi that the elven Queen was his mother for all that; for she was fair of face, and she had only one hand. And he clasped her one hand and kissed it, and kissed her face; and his tears fell upon her face, and she looked amazed. Her features formed themselves into a questioning expression, and she spoke one word: 'Eä', which is Elvish for 'in or at or to this place or position'.

The Elves stood back in wonder; and Queen Lüthwoman herself seemed to register emotion for the first time, for she looked around her with an expression approaching amazement.

'Child,' said one Elf. 'My name is Túrin Againdik-wittingdn, and I lead this band – for as you have heard, our Queen lies under some curse. Yet never has she spoken any word since her madness fell upon her, and now you have lifted Sharon's curse. Who are you?'

'My name is Eärwiggi,' said Eärwiggi. 'And in this woman you call your Queen I recognise my mother, who was married to my father, and who raised me beside the River Optik far to the east of this desolate place. But my parents were commanded by the authority of Sharon into servitude in Blearyland, and they could not resist. How this woman comes to be here I do not know.'

'It is a mystery,' said Túrin. 'For we left Blearyland and came to this shore before Sharon came to this land and victory. We planned to build a boat and sail the Capital Sea, to try and make our way to Wester-supanesse, where we hoped to find a land beyond Sharon's malignancy.'

'We can see the boat,' said Nobbi. 'But it looks to me only half finished.'

'Alas!' cried Túrin.

'Alas!' answered the Elves, and they cast their hoods over their heads.

'Alas?' repeated the Dwarf, in disbelief. 'Come now. Who *says* that? Pull those hoods back, boyos, and stop mincing about. Tell us what happened.'

'We had built half the boat, and looked forward

with hope. But then came a troop of Sharon's soldiers, Orks and beasts, led by a man who bore Sharon's eye in his head. He declared himself the Eye of Sharon, and we could not resist him. His command was a law to our heart, for such is the Dragons' curse. So he ordered us to stop working on the ship, and since then we have been unable to so much as lift a timber to the structure. And he ordered us to prostrate ourselves on the sand, and laughed at us. "Escaping?" he said. "No, you shall not complete your boat, for I order it, and you must obey. And neither do I give you leave to travel any more in Blearyland. But look!" And he laughed again. "There is seaweed to eat, and snow to drink, so you may yet be happy." And so he left, and since he had forbidden us to travel in Blearyland we are stuck here. From time to time he, or one of his kind, stops by as they pass, to laugh at us more.'

'I shall finish your boat,' said Eärwiggi. 'For Sharon's command does not move my heart.'

They were much amazed at this; and yet it proved true. For over the following twelve days, Eärwiggi worked on the boat; and Nobbi helped him. And as the days passed, the land by this portion of seafront thawed, and snowdrops grew, and grass was revealed as the shift of snow withdrew a little. And again the Elves marvelled.

'Truly,' they said, 'the curse of Sharon does not compass you, young Eärwiggi. You are slight in years, but great in power.'

And each night Eärwiggi embraced the elven Queen, and kissed her good night. And every morning she spoke another word.

The first day she said 'Eä!' a second time.

The second day she said 'Eä!' a third time, and Eärwiggi began to fear that it would be her only word, and that her wits were almost as blank as before.

The third day she said 'Se!' And the Elves greatly wondered to hear this, for in Elvish this words means 'utter specified words in a speaking voice'. 'She is amazed at her ability to speak,' declared Túrin. 'As we are! Thus she says this word.'

The fourth day she said 'La!' And the Elves were puzzled, because this meant nothing in Elvish. But Nobbi declared it a word of dwarfish provenance, and suggested that she might be turning into a dwarf; which discomforted the Elves greatly. And they sang mournful songs of bearded queens. But privately Eärwiggi thought it sounded very unlikely.

The fifth day she said, 'Meal!', which means food. And they fed her.

The sixth day she said, 'No!' and looked crossly

upon them. And they were afraid and ashamed, for it is a dire thing when one's monarch looks crossly upon one.

The seventh day she said, 'You!' And they were amazed. 'Me, your majesty?' said Túrin. 'What? What do you want?' But she said nothing more that day.

The eighth day, she said 'Twits!'

The ninth day, she said, 'List!' And Túrin looked sorrowfully, for it seemed to him that his Queen was now simply saying random words.

The tenth day, she said 'En!' and Túrin said, 'What, the letter "n"? That doesn't really make sense.'

The eleventh day, she said, 'To!'

The twelfth day, she said 'Me!' and she pointed at the rocky hills, not far from the beach, which were the westernmost low peaks that grew, moving east, into the Mountain of Byk. But the Elves remained mystified.

And finally the boat was completed, and the Elves thanked Eärwiggi heartily. 'And now we shall leave this land, burdened with the cursed name Blearyland. For although we cannot disobey Sharon, yet his Eye commanded us only to desist from building the boat, and not to travel upon the land, and neither of these things have we done. So we shall hope to reach Westersupanesse, and be free at last from the curse. We say to you: come with us, for your help has been invaluable, really it has.'

But Eärwiggi looked at Nobbi, and said, 'Thanks but no thanks.'

'You sure?' pressed Túrin. 'The land here is cursed. Evil has triumphed. There is nothing to be done but turn our backs on it as a bad job and look for something better.'

'Perhaps,' said Eärwiggi. 'But I still feel I should remain.'

'Then farewell,' said Túrin. 'You have served us well, young Eärwiggi, and one day perhaps we can repay you. Until that time, I urge you to keep your face clean, and always to tell the truth, for these are the badges of Goodness.'

And Eärwiggi smiled, but took this advice with a pinch of salt.

So the Elves made their farewells, and gave Eärwiggi and Nobbi such gifts as they could, and then they pushed the boat from the shore and sailed west, over the horizon. And the last figure Eärwiggi saw was Lüthwoman, Queen of Elves, standing in the prow, or stern – I always get those two mixed up, don't even get me started on port/starboard – anyway, standing at the back of the boat, and waving.

And the thaw had freed a small portion of her mind, such that she recognised Eärwiggi, and smiled at him as she went off. She waved to him with her stump, and then looked at it as if confused for a little space; and then she waved to him with her hand, which was a much better waving device.

And soon they were gone, and the sun followed them over the horizon as if it too were leaving Upper Middle Earth forever.

But the next day came, as next days always do, with a watery sunrise in the skies to the east. And though the whole land laboured under evil tyranny, yet it got on with the business of stirring under the sunshine, to the best of its ability.

And as Nobbi dug tubers from the soil just above the beach, Eärwiggi sat on a stone, and he saw a worrying thing: for a rider on a black horse looked down upon them from a distant hill. He could surely see the green land, like a bite from the otherwise covering snow; and he could see the empty beach, with only a boy and a dwarf by the sea.

And when Eärwiggi looked again, the rider was gone.

Nobbi returned, and the two of them cooked the tubers, and ate them for breakfast. 'Thank heavens,' said the Dwarf, 'them Elves has finally gone. Thought they'd be here forever with their farewells and singing.'

'So,' said Eärwiggi. 'You understood what the Queen was saying, over those twelve days?'

'You'd have to be a moron,' said Nobbi, 'not to understand.'

'Or an Elf,' agreed Eärwiggi. 'Yet I wonder at her words. Can the great Sellāmi truly be here, on this shore, at the very western limit of the mountain chain?'

'Difficult to say really,' said the Dwarf. 'But it's easily checked out, look you.'

So they put on their wolfskins, and made their way over the surface of the deep snow, where it glittered with frozen dew. In an hour of hard walking, sinking their tread into the snow and hauling out each leg to take the next step, they reached the westernmost foothills of the mountain chain, where stark rock dipped down from the spine of peaks eastwards as if a great stone head were reaching to the sea to drink.

The stone presented a blank face to most approaches, yet there was a cave mouth, or so it seemed, where the rock swirled and curled over a black space. So Eärwiggi and Nobbi investigated; and the air inside the cave was cold and sulphurous, and they did not venture inside.

'Here,' called Nobbi. 'Here. Here.' And he pressed himself against the left-hand archway of this cave mouth.

'Where?'

'Inside this rock, look you.'

'*Inside*? How can you tell?'

'Dwarf-knowledge,' said Nobbi.

'I do wish you'd explain it to me.'

'Well,' said Nobbi, feeling his way over the expanse of rock. 'We Dwarfs come into being inside rock, you see. Born there, like. That's what I was doing at the lakeside – I had been quickened, laid if you like, in the rock at the lakeside. Only the lake level must have risen during the time I lay insensate in the stone; and when I broke out, my beard got snagged.'

'That's the story?' said Eärwiggi. 'You told me it was a long story.'

'It is,' said Nobbi. 'Quite. Don't you think?'

'Not really, no.'

'I gave you the shortened version.'

'So you're a newborn? Effectively?'

'Oh we're different to Elves or Men. We're born

with the wisdom of our people already inside us. Anyway, bach, la, look you, never-mind-that-now, what it *means* is that I have a certain *feeling* for stone. It means, for instance, that I know exactly where to smite it—' and he punched the rock hard with his fist, in a sudden motion '—to open it up.' And where Nobbi had punched, the rock split, and inside was the fabled Sellāmi.

They clustered round the opening. 'Oo!' said Eärwiggi.

'Oo,' agreed Nobbi.

'Pick it up,' suggested Eärwiggi.

'*You* pick it up,' said Nobbi. 'It'd have a deleterious effect on me, bach.'

'Deleterious?'

'Trust me.'

So Eärwiggi plucked the Sellāmi from the living rock, and carried it back across the snow field to the beach, by the stream. It felt hot in his hand, and he tucked it inside his wolfskin to keep it safe.

For a while Dwarf and boy sat on the beach beside the stream and debated what to do. But in the midst of their conversation, they heard a yell.

On the far side of the stream was a troop of ork soldiers, together with two – not one, but *two* –

separate Eyes of Sharon, each one mounted on a black horse.

On hearing that a portion of the north-west was free of winter, and that strange things were going on, he had thought to himself: two eyes are better than one eye, and so I shall send my two most potent emissaries to see what is going on.

'You!' called the first Eye of Sharon. 'You!'

And Eärwiggi looked as innocent as he could, and looked over his shoulder, and then tapped himself in the chest as if surprised, and said, 'Me?'

'Yes! What are you doing here?'

'Nothing.'

'You are under the command of Sharon!' called the Second Eye. 'I command you to tell the truth.' But Eärwiggi did not feel this command in his heart, and thought to himself, 'Not likely.'

At this Nobbi stood up and took out his knife. 'Leave him be!' he called. 'He's my friend and I'll not stand by to see him bullied.'

'We have no quarrel with you or your kind, Dwarf,' said the first Eye. 'But we have dominion over all Elves and all Men. Boy! What have you been doing here – speak truthfully.'

And to this command, any Elf or Man would have said: *we have uncovered the fabled Sellāmi from the rocks over there, and here it is.* And the Eye of Sharon would have said, 'Give it me.' And any Elf or Man would have done so. But Eärwiggi did not say this. Instead he scuffed the sand with his foot, and looked sideways, and said, 'Nothing,' in a sulky voice.

'You are our slave,' said the second Eye. 'We will send you to the work-gangs in the south, where you will die of exhaustion, or perhaps survive if you are strong and ruthless, I care not which. But first you will explain to us how you came here.'

At this Nobbi grabbed Eärwiggi in a protective hug. 'If you want him!' he called aloud in the clear air, '*Come* and claim him! If you think you're *hard* enough!' He continued taunting across the little stream. 'Come on then, claim him! Go on. Call that claiming? That's *rubbish*, that is. My *granny* could claim better than that, look you! Yah! You couldn't claim candy from a baby, you lot. He's my mate, bach, and you'll not have him.'

So the Eyes of Sharon splashed over the stream on their fierce black steeds, and the ork warriors trotted after them on foot. They surrounded Nobbi and Eärwiggi the two of them, and the Dwarf was forced to concede, 'Alright, you've come over the stream nice and prompt-like, I suppose that counts as claiming.'

Now the fate of the world hung in the balance. For it occurred to the Eye of Sharon to kill the boy there and then, just because he was in a bad mood. And had he done this, then Blearyland would have languished under the Sharonny until the ending of time. But he did not kill him; he stayed his hand, although not from mercy; but the death toll in Upper Middle Earth had been rather high lately, and it was getting harder to find slaves to make up the numbers of the work gangs. And so Eärwiggi was spared.

And the Eyes of Sharon did not bother to bind Eärwiggi's arms, for they were confident of the power of the Dragons' magic to hold him to his will. Instead the first Eye addressed the Dwarf. 'Sir Dwarf, our quarrel is not with you. Go, and leave us to our business with our slave here.'

'Well,' said Nobbi, rubbing his beard. 'I don't think so.'

'Look over there!' called the second Eye. 'The boat has gone!' And he spurred his horse and rode over the beach, to the place where the elvish boat had been constructed. Its keelprint was still in the sand, and spare timber and tools were piled by the grasses at the head of the beach.

The second Eye galloped back along the beach to

the place where Eärwiggi stood. 'Do you know any-thing of this? Answer me truly.'

'No,' said Eärwiggi, grinning.

'There is strange work here,' said the second Eye. 'There were Elves here, and they had been forbidden either to complete their boat, or to travel anywhere in the land. So where are they?'

'Perhaps,' said the first Eye, 'they pulled their incomplete boat into the water in despair and drowned themselves?' He said this with an almost hopeful inflection of voice.

'Possibly,' said the first Eye. 'Although I have never heard of Elves committing suicide before.'

Nobbi cleared his throat loudly. It was a tremend-ous, rumbling, thrumming throat-clearing, such as only Dwarfs can properly manage. It sounded like scree falling down a great slope. 'Right, boyos,' he said, pulling himself to his full height, which by coincidence was exactly the same height as Eärwiggi. 'Now, you two – I've a question, and I want to address it to Sharon himself.'

'Speak to me,' said the first Eye. 'Verily I *am* Sharon, wearing this mannish body as a tool.'

'No,' said the second Eye, crossly. 'Speak to *me*. I am the true Sharon.'

'I was here first,' said the first Eye.

'And *I* was created Eye of Sharon before you,' said the second Eye. 'Talk to me, Sir Dwarf, and Sharon will answer your question.'

'No, Sir Dwarf,' said the first Eye. 'Ignore this man – he is a merely secondary, subsidiary Eye. I'm the one you should address.'

'Me!' yelled the second Eye.

'*He* said,' said Eärwiggi, pointing to the first Eye. And at that moment, as in the dead eye of a storm, everything fell silent, so that his words could be heard by all: the Orks ceased their mutterings; the sea surf seemed to hush to silence; the wind dropped away; and the two bickering Eyes were speechless with their respective rages. And so Eärwiggi spoke, and rarely have any words spoken by a child been so significant. The words of Túrin returned to him: *always tell the truth and something about the face*, because actually Eärwiggi couldn't remember the second part. And he thought of the Sellāmi tucked into his clothes. And he spoke.

'*He* said,' said Eärwiggi, pointing to the first Eye, 'that he was going to kill you. I overheard him.'

There was a moment of silence. The fate of the world turned on its pivot.

'Oh you *did*, did you?' roared the second Eye.

'No!' called the first Eye in outrage. 'What? Hey –
no.'

'Do you know that doesn't surprise me at *all*,' said
the second Eye.

'What are you talking about?'

'I always thought you were a murderous swine,'
said the second Eye. 'And I don't mean that in a good
way.'

'You take that back!' said the first Eye, livid. 'You
just apologise and take that back right now!'

'You're *plotting to kill me*,' said the second Eye.

'No I'm not,' snarled the first Eye. 'Though heaven
knows you deserve it.'

'The boy has a command upon him to tell the
truth!' cried the second Eye with furious emphasis.
'Can you deny it? – It is the Dragons' magic.' He
turned to Eärwiggi. 'Boy, speak again, and speak
only the truth. Did this creature say he was going to
slay me?'

'Oh yes,' said Eärwiggi. 'When you rode over the
beach a moment ago. He said "When I come back.
I'm going to stick him with my long black sword."
And he called you a rude name.'

'Oo, I never!' yelled the first Eye. 'He's lying!'

'He has the *Dragons' spell* upon him,' shrieked
the second Eye. 'He *cannot* lie! You, however, are

composed of *nothing but* lies and treachery. Since being appointed one of the Eyes of Sharon you have spent the entire time plotting to rise up against your own Master.'

'How could I plot like that?' howled the first Eye, in an ecstasy of rage and fury. 'I am not Sharon's servant, but part of Sharon himself. You talk gibberish. Your brain must have rotted away – are your wits truly so maggot-eaten that you would think . . .'

In a trice, the second Eye whipped out his black-bladed sword and sheathed it again in the first Eye's chest. The victim's eyes opened even wider and looked even more furious, which Eärwiggi would hardly have believed possible, although there it was, for all to see. His speech broke off in mid word with a gurgle, and he fell straight out of his saddle to the damp sand.

The Orks sucked in a collective 'Ha!' of horror, and all took a step back.

The second Eye looked with surprise at the sword in his hand. Vapours curled off the blade, and a dribble of blood ran from the point. 'Er,' he said.

At exactly that moment the ground shook violently.

❊

Eärwiggi was thrown off his feet by the tremor; and even the stocky, sturdy Dwarf had a job not falling over. The Orks squealed in terror, and fled away, some south, some east. The body of the slain Eye of Sharon twitched on the sand as if going through a second death spasm.

The second Eye's horse reared up, and sloughed him off backwards, before cantering whinnyingly away over the dune grass and onto the snow. And the second Eye lay screaming.

The ground shook a second time.

The sea seemed to boil, and throw up exaggerated waves, twice or three times as tall as they had been only a moment before. For a third time the ground shook.

Eärwiggi got on all fours and looked north. The cave where they had found the Sellāmi had collapsed. The rocks above were shaking, trembling, rearing in great spasms, as if the mountains themselves were feverish.

Getting to his feet, the second Eye looked around him with fear and horror on his face. His eyes were black and sightless, and he stumbled. 'Something is very wrong here . . .' he said.

And with the mightiest tremor yet the mountains burst to life, and upreared into the air. The second Eye screamed and fell on his face.

'It is the ending of all things!' said Eärwiggi.

'Now let's not *leap* to conclusions,' said Nobbi, before his voice was drowned out by a tempestuous rushing of wind. The sea's edge sucked back and ran away from them, withdrawing half a league to reveal wet mud and seaweeds and gasping fish dancing in plain air.

A shadow passed over them; and the Dragon of the North, awake again, was circling very slowly through the air over their heads.

The Dragon of the North spoke: 'What is your name?' And his voice boomed and rumbled, as the earth shivered its last trembles and settled itself.

To begin with, Eärwiggi thought he must be speaking to somebody else. He prodded Nobbi's shoulder, and nodded at him, raising his eyebrows, as if to say 'Go on then.' But the Dwarf said, 'He's speaking to *you*, bach.'

So Eärwiggi said, 'Eärwiggi.'

'You have the Sellāmi?'

Eärwiggi thought about telling another lie; but then he thought to himself 'If I lie all the time, then people will know the truth simply by inverting what I say. So I shall tell the truth on this occasion.' He looked up at the huge beast. It hung in the sky above the beach, filling the view; although at the edges of his great rock-like frame Eärwiggi could see the sky behind. It looked darker, and clouds were hurrying over it at a great rate as if keen to get away.

'Yes,' he replied. 'Do you want it?'

'No,' said the Dragon. 'It was in my claw, but it froze me to the margin of Upper Middle Earth – as you saw. I cannot carry it, as I hoped.'

'Carry it?'

'Away.' And he swum through the air in a circle, nodding his great head at the west. 'It should not be here. It disturbs the balance of this world. We are ready to pay the price to be rid of it.'

'We?' asked Eärwiggi.

'My brother dragons,' said the Dragon of the North. 'The time has come.'

'I don't understand.'

'Sharon hoped to form an unbreakable spell. He took much of our power from us to fashion the spell, and its words are our words, and they are words of making. He commanded that he be lord over all Elves and Men; and that he be invulnerable to harm; and that he be immortal; and that he be victorious in any battle. And with these words he has enslaved Upper Middle Earth, for they are powerful words.'

'But,' said Nobbi, with a great smile on his face, 'You, laddo, have resisted his magic!'

'Your mother was an elf, and your father a man,' boomed the Dragon. 'And you are both elvish and mannish, and yet neither. As neither man nor elf, Sharon could not command you.'

'Even the winter thawed around you,' said Nobbi.

'The problem with a being such as Sharon,' said the Dragon, 'is that he can only see the one thing or the other. He must inhabit the centre, and margins make him uncomfortable. If looked at in terms of *one thing* or *the other thing* his charm was firm. But here, at the margins of the world, it frays.'

'Frays?'

'The Eye of Sharon is both Sharon and not-Sharon, for he is a Man possessed by Sharon. Sharon cannot be harmed, or killed, or defeated in battle; and so the second Eye was victorious, and alive, and unharmed. But *Men* can be harmed, or killed, or defeated in battle; and so the first Eye lies dead. And the first Eye was Sharon, also, and so the spell is broken.'

'Is it so simple?' asked Eärwiggi.

'No,' boomed the Dragon, mournfully.

'Sharon fought Sharon!' chortled the dwarf. 'Both must be victorious by the terms of the spell, and yet both *cannot* be victorious – for to be victorious means to defeat the other. The spell circled back on itself, a serpent devouring its own tail! It *fused* itself.'

'Is the spell broken?' Eärwiggi asked again. 'Just like that?'

'No,' boomed the Dragon, 'and yes, for this is the way of all answers to the really complicated questions.'

'How do you mean?'

'The spell is made of our magic, and of our words; and the world itself is made of our magic and of our words. The spell is broken, and not broken. It is broken, in that Sharon no longer commands the hearts of Men or Elves, and he can be harmed and slain and defeated in battle. But it is not broken, so long as the world is unbroken; and some part of Sharon remains immortal, imperishable, invincible. So mighty a spell cannot simply disappear in a puff of smoke. Its unmaking will unmake the land that we made; and it will unmake us also, for we are the speech that spoke the land, just as we are the speech that spoke the spell.'

'Well, this is most alarming news,' said Eärwiggi. 'It sounds, after all, like the end of the world.'

'End,' said the Dragon, 'and beginning. The tremors are starting now, in the heart of Blearyland;

and they will soon reach us here at the edge of things. Already Sharon's tower has fallen in rubble, and his Thing™ has fallen from him and been washed away in the flood, to fall from sight and mind. Already his Orks flee in terror or fall into chasms in the earth. Soon the land will be broken, hills will tumble into valleys, fields will rear up as new mountains, and everything will become new. Yet Men and Elves will survive, and the new world will continue.'

'Dear me,' said Eärwiggi. 'What a to-do.'

'It is indeed,' boomed the Dragon, lifting his head to the hurtling clouds and the wine-dark sky, 'a To-Do! We shall soon perish, broken to fragments by the upheavals of this land we made.'

'Oh. I'm sorry to hear that.'

'Don't worry. We have laid our eggs in the rocks of this world, and a new generation of Dragons will arise eventually, smaller than we but more removed from the evil of Moregothic who created us, and wiser in their way. We accept our fate. Will you now accept yours?'

'My fate?'

'You must carry the Sellámi over the western ocean, and return it to Emu who made it.'

'But there isn't time to build a boat!' said

Eärwiggi. And truly it seemed so, for the hills on the horizon were shuddering like jellies, and trees and rocks were bouncing into the air; and the air was bruised with the distant sound of apocalypse.

'Climb onto my tail,' said the Dragon, whisking his huge rocky tail through the air and laying it along the beach. 'Quick now.'

As Eärwiggi clambered up he asked, 'Will you carry me through the air?'

'Not I,' boomed the Dragon. 'I cannot leave this land I created, and the Sellāmi is too heavy a thing for my power. But you can take it in your hand. By cutting off the end of it, Sharon opened its magic potency; for it is full of light and power. Hold it tight, with the severed end towards the ground.'

'Alright,' said Eärwiggi, doing so. 'Then what?'

'You'll see,' said the Dragon. And he lifted his tail into the air again.

'Goodbye!' Eärwiggi called down to Nobbi on the ground. 'It was nice knowing you.'

'Glad to know you too,' said the Dwarf. But Eärwiggi was already high in the air, and the world beneath had shrunk away.

From here he could see the great spread of lands to the east, and the stippled deserts of ocean water to the west. And it was a vantage point from which the spreading wave of earthquake destruction was clearly visible, shaking the whole landscape; as if the fields and hills and mountains were made not of solid substance, but of a sluggish fluid, and a great wave was passing through them, undoing and remaking.

The Dragon whipped his tail round; and with a tumbling sense of falling in his belly, Eärwiggi dropped hundreds of yards; yet still he clutched onto the Sellāmi.

And with sudden and devastating force, the Dragon of the North whipped his tail round again and hurled Eärwiggi westward into the air. He screamed. He couldn't help it. He was flying free like a chucked pebble, with the seas wrinkling far below him.

And with a great shudder, the Sellāmi came to life in his hands. Light gushed from its severed end: light of all colours, streaking behind him as he flew: a comet's tail of red and gold, of spring green and sky blue.

He flew so fast that the wind tugged at his face, pulling his mouth open and squeezing his eyes shut; and he could no longer hear himself call. But ducking his head down and forcing his eyes open, he saw the path of many colours he was marking across the sky. And even in his fear he was amazed.

And from the ground those Elves and Men who survived the upheavals of their world looked up in amazement also. Never before had such a thing been seen in Upper Middle Earth. And at first it was called 'Eärwiggi-in-the-sky'; but afterwards, when people thought back and decided this was a pretty silly name for it they called it instead 'rainbow'.

Eärwiggi flew, and the force and noise of the air pressed him close about, but still he cut his way through the sky.

Behind him the Dragon of the North broke into ten thousand fragments of stone, some great boulders, some small shards, and scattered across the landscape; and Nobbi did call out 'Crikey o' bikey' and hide his head; and by great good fortune, or perhaps by good fate, none of the ten thousand fragments fell upon him.

And in like fashion did each of the four great dragons perish with the breaking up of this, their greatest spell.

Eärwiggi passed through the highest point of the sky, where the blue aether was close enough almost for him to touch; and below him the sea was ever more distant, and the curve of the world was clearly visible. The sun's light and heat was strong upon this place, and one thought crossed his mind; that he was the most alone and free of any Upper Middle Earthly individual.

And then he began to fall in a great arc. But although the fall curved down and down, yet as he clutched the Sellāmi it seemed to Eärwiggi that his speed was slowing, and that he was less falling and more floating, until he caught a glimpse of a fresh green landscape, and the crisp frill of white breakers on a golden beach, and then he plopped onto the turf of Asdar.

'Wow. *That*,' he said to nobody in particular, 'was quite a ride.'

So it was that the Sellāmi was returned to Asdar. Of Eärwiggi little more is known; some tales say he lived in happiness in Asdar forever; other tales say he returned to Upper Middle Earth, to find a changed landscape and new adventures. But of Sharon all the tales agree: he was cast down in the ruin of his orgulous castle, and his spirit fled whimpering to the high sky where it was lost to memory. And his Thing™, the last remnant of the Sellāmi in Upper Middle Earth, fell into floodwater and was washed away, whither none knew.

And Men and Elves rebuilt their cities from the

ruins of the land. And the name of Blearyland was wiped from official records, for all agreed it had brought nothing but bad luck; and instead the land was called Elfriardor. Or Manland, according to some. Or Dwarfswereherefirstshire according to others.

So ends the tale of Eärwiggi.[26]

---

26 Whose name, clearly, is not derived from the Elvish for 'ear covering' after all, but from the Old Mannish meaning 'air-way' or 'air-path', on account of his fantastic journey through the sky.

## The Voyage of the Darned Traitor

During that time when the whole of Upper Middle Earth was overrun by darkness and Sharon was Master of All Things, certain Elves, called for obvious reasons the Coward Elves, fled to the far north and west of Blearyland. And there they built themselves a boat, called by them *The Spirit of Exploration*, but called by everybody who remained behind and lived under the terrible yoke of Sharon *The Spirit of the Darned Traitor*.

As Sharon laid waste to Blearyland, Túrin Againdikwittingdn took his people, and escorted the vacant-headed Queen Lüthwoman to the uttermost western shore of Upper Middle Earth. There they began building a boat, but the construction fell under the malign influence of one of the Eyes of Sharon, who came upon them. And they fell at his feet as he ordered them to cease building the boat, and ordered them also not to roam the land but to waste the rest of their days sitting on the cold beach. And they were powerless to resist his command, and languished on the beach for many months.

But to their aid came Eärwiggi of the Mighty Fib; and being half-elven and half-mannish he was un-affected by Sharon's magic, and he completed the boat on their behalf. And they thanked him and bade him farewell, and sailed away to the west.

The voyage lasted many weeks, through storms and over calm seas, under glassy skies and under cloud that drooped low enough to envelop them. Beneath the keel of their boat the unsatisfied surge sucked with importunate lip, and threatened several times to swallow them whole; but they stayed true of heart, and steered the *Darned Traitor* west, always west. 'And at the end,' said Túrin Againdikwittingdn, 'we shall arrive at the coast of Westersupanesse, the paradise of Asdar.'

But he was unaware that Emu, annoyed by pre-vious evil incursions, had rerouted the route that led over the surface of the sea through an inter-dimensional gate to another place.

And after long voyaging, the mariners thought they saw the end of the ocean; and the horizon of the sea glimmered with a strange light, green and pink. And the sky greyed, and storm clouds collided above them with great crumpling crashing noises. Lightning twigged flickeringly across the darkness. Rain filled the air all around with plummeting water;

and everything was soaked; and the waves began to tip and heave. And as Túrin called his crew to the deck a twisting tunnel of black wind engulfed the ship.

They were wrenched, as it seemed, full out of the sea and thrown high in the air; and yet, at the same time, they felt motionless and the wind and rain fell away. A strange quiet was all around them. Túrin, gasping, his wet clothes steaming in the newly dry air and his hair standing strangely on end, stood on the deck and looked at what had become of the world around them. It seemed as though they were in a long tunnel formed by the twisting arcing lines of a whirlwind; yet it was perfectly still and perfectly quiet. So close did the walls of this tunnel seem to be that Túrin thought he could reach out and touch them; but when he did they crackled and snarled with shards of light, and he felt a jarring jolt up his arm that left his limb numb for many minutes.

But then the tunnel fell away from them on all sides, and the *Darned Traitor* found itself floating again in water; and on either side were green fields; and soon they drifted underneath a stone bridge. And they found themselves in a populous city, with houses and shops of stone, and many people crowding the stone-set paths, and curious carts that moved without horses.

And they docked, and wandered the strange city. 'Are we in Westersupanesse?' asked the Coward Elves.

'We must be,' said Túrin. 'This must be paradise.'

And they were surprised, frankly, that paradise had quite so many bicycles. To say nothing of the buses. But it doesn't do to query the inscrutable designs of providence, or risk the wrath of Emu, so the Coward Elves wandered around for a while. And when they returned to their ship it had been impounded by the municipal authorities for non-payment of moorage charges.

And over many years in paradise the Coward Elves eventually settled down and Túrin Againdik-wittingdn opened a small tobacconist's just off Saint Giles, and lived there with Queen Lúthwoman; and the other Coward Elves lived in various places, some in the university, some in other towns. And of their various lives, nothing more is told in this tale.

# Part 3

# The History of the
# War of the Thing™

[*Editor's note*. My grand-uncle's notes towards *Lowered Off the Rings*, his gymnasium-set allegory for the great War of the Thing™, indicate the extent to which his publisher and himself were keen to introduce the mythology of Upper Middle Earth to as many people as possible, or as George-Ann Allen Nonwin put it, 'to milk every last purple cent outta this baby.' He and my grand-uncle experimented with recasting the material in various forms, and various media; some of which are illustrated below.]

### *Letters between A. R. R. R. Roberts and George-Ann Allen Nonwin.* **Lowered Off the Rings** *takes shape.*

My grand-uncle had been working on tales set in his Fantasy world for many decades without ever interesting a publisher. He regularly sent out portions of the MS to all the publishers he could think of, and regularly received rejection letters, usually by return of post. Indeed, his breakfast was ruined unless he had one or two really good rejection letters to ponder over his Sultana Bran. 'I find a rejection letter to be better than the best commercially produced laxative available on the market,' he once told me.

But all that changed when my father met the publisher George-Ann Allen Nonwin. 'A curious fellow,' A R R R R wrote to a friend shortly after he first met the publisher for lunch. 'It seems that his parents had been unable to reconcile a certain argument over whether "George" or "Ann" was the better name for a child.' Nonwin accepted the manuscript of *The Soddit* for publication, and commissioned

Dunglewis Carroll to illustrate it. The book was, of course, enormously successful, and spent no fewer than two weeks in the 'Hardback Illustrated Fiction for Children Published by a London Publisher in Red Covers Top Ten Bestselling Books' Bestseller List, at No 9 and No 10 respectively.

Nonwin, naturally, wanted my grand-uncle to pen a sequel to this successful book, and suggested an adventure narrative concerning the Ultimate Battle of Good Versus Evil, with the Awful Sharon battling the forces of Men and Elves. With some soddits in it. But my grand-uncle, used to the specialised demands of academic scholarship, found it hard to adjust to the requirements of commercial publishing. In the early stages he was compelled to ask George-Ann for assistance. If this galled his sense of pride to a certain extent, then matters were not helped by Nonwin's sometimes brusque tone.

*George-Ann Allen Nonwin Publishers,*
Tuesday 19<sup>th</sup>. Morning. About eleven o'clock. Well, eleven-oh-four if you want me to be – eleven-oh-five, it just flipped over as I was writing that last bit.

Dear A R R R R,

Re: the Big Fantasy Sequel. You tell me you are having some trouble with the conceptual framework of this. Come, my dear fellow, it's child's play.

It must be a thousand-page epic spanning a whole continent with a *dramatis personae* including many scores of characters. The narrative must concern the very biggest topics, the battle of Good against ultimate Evil, the importance of free will, the seductive power of wickedness and so on. Naturally, in framing such a story, you will need to consider *not only* individual items of personal jewellery but personal accessories and adornment in general. I advise you to build the story around a single magic item of gold frippery.

Sincerely,

George-Ann

Dear George-Ann

Thank you for your very helpful suggestions.

A R R R R

My grand-uncle followed his publisher's advice, and attempted to recast his mythic material around some fictional component. After several weeks racking his brains he lighted on the conception of a magic ring that renders its owner invisible. Nonwin, however, queried the logic of this conception.

My dear A, Of course (it is, after all, self-evident) any thousand-page heroic Fighting Fantasy trilogy dramatising the bloodsoaked ultimate battle of Good against Evil, must be constructed around an item of jewellery. So far so good. But why, old boy, have you lighted upon a *ring* that renders its wearer *invisible to others*? I'm afraid I just don't see the logic. Why should a *finger-ring* render you invisible? A magic golden monocle, maybe – The Monocle of Sorrow, perhaps? Spectacles at a pinch.

    G

In the event, A R R R R worked on the monocle idea for seven anguished months, before finally and reluctantly abandoning it. It crops up in many early drafts of the first volume; but after much labour he decided that it was artistically unsustainable.

Dear G-A-A,

    I confess I've had, finally, to abandon The Monocle of Sorrow. And, of course, it would be absurd to revert to the 'Magic Finger-ring of Invisibility'. Might I prevail upon you for an opinion as to which of the following looks most promising?

    The Earrings of Doom!
    The Bellybutton Stud of Evil!

The Wristwatch of Terror!
The Brooch of Disaster!
The Tiny Gold Dolphin On An Eighteen-Carat
   Chain of Misery!
The Medallion of Ultimate Evil!

I have also been rethinking the choice of titles for the three constituent books. I feel that, to be in keeping with our democratic age, I should downplay the heroic kingliness of the original titles, and choose something with which citizens of a modern democracy will identify. Please notify the printers to reset all proofs with the following titles:

1. The Fellowship of the Single Transferable Vote
2. The Two Funding Authorities
3. The Return of the Democratically Elected Upper
   Chamber

The overall title should be *Lord of Bling*.
Best wishes for Easter, A

Nonwin pressed for the Brooch of Disaster, but A R R R R found that the notion of a single evil earring had seized his imagination. He rewrote chapter seven 'Eighteen Carats of Catastrophe' with a brooch, but didn't like the result. As he explained himself to Nonwin:

After much consideration I've had to abandon the brooch. I have to say I feel that my Earrings of Inadibility are a *much* stronger artistic conceit. Let me pick, for example, one moment from many from my thousands of pages of manuscript, to illustrate how dramatic and exciting this piece of personal adornment could be.

*The Fell Walkers of Fell Darkness were upon them, their great black coats and black boots crunching upon the dead pine needles. Freudo stumbled backwards, and before he knew what he was doing he had slipped the Earrings of Doom upon his earlobes. With horror he saw the King of the Fell Walkers stride close and closer to Sham's sleeping form. 'Sham!' he cried, 'Sham! Look out! Rouse yourself, Sham, and flee! Fly! Flee!' But, of course, the Earrings had rendered him wholly inaudible.*

You see? To rewrite that scene with a brooch would be to lose all dramatic excitement. I do hope you agree.

Sincerely,

A R R R R

A week later my grand-uncle wrote the following note, which demonstrates how strained relations with his publisher had become.

George-Ann,

I called your office several times yesterday by telephone, only to be told that you were 'out at lunch'. Do you really expect me to believe that a publisher could be out at lunch *from eleven-twenty in the morning until nearly three in the afternoon*? Pah – pah I say. No conceivable lunch, in any profession, could take so long. Clearly you were avoiding me. I will confess that I am hurt and distressed by your evasion.

A.

PS: I hear on the grapevine that the Baroness Orczy is presently working on a three thousand page Heroic Fantasy based on a magical Naked-Lady-Tattoo of Power, drawn in the biceps of the central character. If she can get away with that notion, I really don't see how my Earrings of Doom can be denied me.

As late as March, A R R R R was still battling Nonwin over the precise shape his central Decorative Golden Adornment of Catastrophe should take. A series of letters from June of the same year illustrate how passionate each man was on the subject.

*The 'Snug', Covent Garden,*
Thursday afternoon

My dear R,

Go for the brooch. Earring is plain silly.

With very warmest and best wishes,

George-Ann

*Suburbia, Friday*

Dear G-A,

No it isn't.

Sincerest wishes,

A R R R Roberts

*George-Ann Allen Nonwin Publishers,*
Tuesday

Dear R,

Thank you for your communication of the 17th inst. Yes it is.

Sincerely,

George-Ann

*Suburbia,*
Thursday

Dear George,

No, it isn't.

With warmest regards, and best wishes for yourself and your family,

ARRRR

*George-Ann Allen Nonwin Publishers,*
Monday

Dear R,
Yes it *is*.
Sincerely,
George-Ann


*Suburbia,*
Thursday 30th

Dear George,
No, it isn't.
best, A


*George-Ann Allen Nonwin Publishers,*
Friday 31st

Dear R,
Yes it is, and before you reply, let me add: yes it is.
You're a stubborn, brick-headed idiotic twit of a man.
You smell. I find myself compelled to utter impolite
speculations concerning your mother. You kissed a
dog once. You enjoyed it. You've never kissed a girl.
You're stupid and you smell. You run like a midget.
You bite your nails.
With heartfelt regards,
George-Ann Allen Nonwin

*Suburbia,*
Wednesday 3<sup>rd</sup>

Dear George,
  Listen to me: No, It Isn't.
  best, A

*George-Ann Allen Nonwin Publishers,*
Saturday morning

Dear R,
  I'm sorry to say that I was unable to read your last communication, because after opening the letter I was forced to put my hands over my eyes and go *wa!-wa!-wa!-wa!-wa!* at the top of my voice. I must therefore conclude, without evidence to the contrary, that you concur in my judgment that, yes, it is.
  George-A

*Suburbia,*
Monday 8<sup>th</sup>

Dear George,
  You're a child.
  sincerely, A

*George-Ann Allen Nonwin Publishers,*
Tuesday 9<sup>th</sup>

Dear R,
  *You* are, you mean.
  George-Ann

*Suburbia,*
Wednesday 10<sup>th</sup>

Dear George,
    I know *you* are, but what am I?
    sincerely, A

*George-Ann Allen Nonwin Publishers,*
Thursday 11<sup>th</sup>

Dear Sir,
    George-Ann Nonwin is out of the office today, and
will deal with your enquiry on his return.
    Sincerely,
    Jill Philips, pp. G-A Nonwin

A postal strike terminated the correspondence at this
point.

# *Farmer Greenegs of Ham*

[*Editor's note*: this manuscript, an early draft of my grand-uncle's *Lowered Off the Rings* work, has recently been discovered in the Ballsiol archives. Instructed to provide a sequel for his children's book *The Soddit*, A. R. R. Roberts initially pitched his sequel at an even younger demographic. The manuscript is illustrated with preliminary sketches by Dr Douglas Zeus]

p.1    'I do not like this Magic Ring
         I do not like it, Sam-old-thing.'

p.2    'Would you like it in the Shire?'

        'I would not, could not in the Shire,
        I do not like its words of fire.
        I do not like this Magic Ring,
        I do not *like* it, Sam-old-thing.'

p.3    'Say—
              In the dark?
        Here in the dark?
        Would you, could you, in the dark?'

## The Sellamillion

'Sam, I'll tell you this in actual fact—
I hate this magic artefact;
I do not like it in the dark
I will not treat it as a lark
Not in a field, not in a barrow
Not in a mountain pass that's narrow
Not in a broader mountain pass
I'd sooner kiss your hairy

p.4   Toes
I *do not like* this Magic Ring
I *do not like* it, Sam-old-thing.'

p.5   'Here
At Mount Doom?
Here, up Old Doom?
Will you be wearing it any time soon?'

'I do not like this ring of power
I do not like it *any* hour.
I do not like it here, or there,
It is not something I will wear.'

p.6   'Here in the third volume?
Now! In the third volume—
Could you, would you? Can it be
That you'll give way in volume 3?'

'I *did not like* it in volume one.
Nor in the volume that's just gone.
I do not like it in *this* volume.
Any more than being chased by Golume.
Not with Departure nor Return of King
I do not *like* this Magic Ring.'

p.7  'You say it's what you can't abide.
Try it – try it – *then* decide.
Try, before committing ringicide.'

p.8  'Say!'

p.9  'I *like* this Evil Ring.
I do! I like the awful thing!

And I *will* wear it on my finger!
And I *will* be apocalypse-bringer!
And I *will* drive my allies mad!
It is *so good*, to be so very bad!
I'll use it to bring blight and woe
From wizard's peak to dwarfish toe.
To shift from seen into unseen,
To turn bread blue and hens-eggs green,
And generally make mortals glum.
Thank you!
Thank you!
Sam-old-chum.'

[Later that year, Nonwin persuaded my grand-uncle to write up some of his personal mythology in more populist form. The first fruit of this new resolution was the script of a situation comedy, which Roberts hoped to sell to the BBC. Filming was not completed on the pilot episode, and only this portion remains.]

## *Ent's Army*

**Theme**:
*Who do you think you are kidding, Mister Sauron*
*If you think Old Forest's done —*
*We are the trees that'll hoomm hoooooooommm hmm.*
*Hmmm.*
*We are hmmmmmmmm.*
[pause: 7 minutes]

*Mr Elm goes off to the Haradvale on*
*The 821-*
*year old drover's path —*
*But he comes home each evening*
*And he's ready with his gum* (exuded-from-a-small-incision-in-his-bark)

*So*
*Who do you think you are kidding, Mister Sauron*
*If you think Old Forest's —*
*Hmmmmmmmmmm.*
*Hom, hoom, hmmm.*

**Scene**: *The Old Forest. Many trees. Enter* CAPTAIN MAINBEARDING, SERGEANT WISDEN, CORPORAL JUNIPER, PRIVATE POPLAR.

CAPTAIN MAINBEARDING: Pay attention trees. I'm afraid the Orks are – hooom, hoooomm, hoom-mmmm. [*dozes for twenty minutes*] Ah! Yes, the Orks are – hmmm – presently setting fire to my lower branches.

CORPORAL JUNIPER: [*speaking very slowly in a deep bass-baritone*] Do-oo-ooo-o-o-oo-oo —o—oo—on't . . . pa—aa—a-aaa—

PRIVATE POPLAR: Mr Mainbearding! [*pause: 3 minutes*] Mr Mainbearding! [*pause: 7 minutes*]

CORPORAL JUNIPER: —aa—a-aaa—a-a-a—a—

PRIVATE POPLAR: Mr Mainbearding! An ork para-trooper has fallen – hoom – into my branches – hmmm hmmm – and is now dangling from them.

Dangling, he is. What – hmm – what shall I do, Mr Mainbearding?

CAPTAIN MAINBEARDING: [*shaking his head slowly*] You stupid sapling.

CORPORAL JUNIPER: —aa-a-nn—nic! Do—oo-oo-o —o-o-oo—oo . . . [*His roots settle into the soft loam and he goes to sleep*]

SERGEANT WISDEN: [*observing* JUNIPER] Ah, the sweet rainwater-sodden earth, the life-giving water of the ground. He does like it up him.

# *The Adventures of Tommy Bythewho*

[*Editor's Note*: Very little remains of my grand-uncle's abortive attempt to recast the material of *Lowered Off the Rings* as a rock opera, tentatively entitled *Ring, Ring, Why Don't You Give Me A Greatly-Lengthened-Though-Horribly-Attenuated-Life-of-Gnawing-Anxiety-and-Maniacal-Possessiveness*.[27] Of the original forty songs, only a dozen or so were ever recorded; the Earls Court Spectacular, performed with full band and backing orchestra on ice, closed after only three months, and the soundtrack album only reached number six in the album charts, selling a pitiful 600,000 copies]

**Song:** *Tis balls, Wizard*

Ever since I was a young lad I've been Aryan blonde
   and tall
From Mirkjaggawood down to Fanguverymuchhorn,
   I'm the prettiest elf of all,

---

27   Later retitled *Bing Sings 'Rings'*.

But I've not seen anything like him in any elven hall,
That Tommy Bythewho-oh
He hardly fits this tale at all —

> *Duh-duh, duhh, duhh, d-duhh,*
> *Duh-duh, duhh, duhh, d-duhh.*[28]

He stands like a hippy, he'll smoke almost anything,
Hardly ever speaks in prose, he much prefers to sing,
Doesn't care for money, unmoved by its kerching,
That Tom Bonglemmehaveago
Sure isn't affected by the Evil Ring —

> *Duh-duh, duhh, duhh, d-duhh,*
> *Duh-duh, duhh, duhh, d-duhh.*[29]

He's an authorial symbol,
He isn't like the rest
          of the characters
He's a strange anachronism
And he wears a velvet vest.

He lives in an oddly stylised version of the nineteen-
     sixties even though this tale is supposed to be

---

28   Elvish. Translation: 'Yes, yes, oh very much so, yes, indeed,/Yes, yes,
oh very much so, yes indeed; *oh* yes.'

29   Elvish. Translation: 'No, No he's not, certainly no, no,/nope, not in
the slightest, oh no, what on earth gave you that idea, certainly not, no.'

timeless and was in fact written between the
nineteen-teens and 1950s,
Apparently very important to the author, although
few readers complain if these Scenes are cut clean
out from the movie on account of the narratively
thrifty s-
    elections of the director,
That Tommy Bythewho-oh,
He don't hardly fit this tale at all.

He's a transparent allegory,
Of a rural English idyll
But in terms of characterisation
He's a load of twaffling piddle.

Other songs composed by my grand-uncle for this
Musical Interlude included:

- *Tom Bythewho Prelude: Wap-dang-a-dingle-doh-a-derry-down-the-dongle-dung*
- *'I'm Free! And Freedom Tastes of Not Having To Spend Seven Years Filming in New Zealand'*
- *'See Me, Hear Me, Feel Me (Not in the Movie Version You Won't)'*
- *'I'm your Wicked Uncle Ernie, Interfering with Young Children, and I'll Make You Very Uncomfortable Indeed When, in Twenty*

*Years' Time, the Composer is Arrested for Internet Child Porn Offences and You Look Back on This Song And Think, Blimey, That Puts Things In An Unpleasant New Light, Doesn't It?'*

- *'Talking 'Bout My Sellamillion'*
- *'Boromir, Boroyur (ah-haa)'*
- *'Moria – I've Just Seen a Mine Called Moria'*
- *'Gimli, Gimli, Gimli, A Dwarf After Midnight'*
- *'(She Told Me To) Ork This Way'*
- *Tom Bythewho Rousing Conclusive Chorus: Wap-dang-a-dingle-doh-derry-down-the-dongle-dung (reprise)*

Soundtrack available on 'His Evil Master's Voice'/ Nonwin-recordings.

## *Under Mirk Wood: a Play for Voices*
**By Bob Dylan Thomas Boombadillo**

**First Dwarf:** To begin at the beginning: a small wood, under the starlight, look you, bach, though they go mad they shall go into that good night, dumb, and fuse the green under apple boughs, bach, la, dew.

**Second Dwarf (Molly):** [*falsetto*] That giant spider kissed me!

**Third Dwarf (Gomer):** [*baritone*] Kissed you?

**Molly:** [*falsetto*] Underneath the branches.

**Gomer:** [*baritone*] Underneath the branches?

**Molly:** [*falsetto*] He was trying to fill my veins with poison, wrap me up and lay eggs in me, and all for the sake of love.

**Gomer:** [*baritone*] All bite and no bark, some spiders. All bark and no bite, some trees.

**Molly:** [*falsetto*] O love! Spider love.

**Gomer:** [*falsetto*] Nothing sweeter.

**Molly:** [*baritone*] Afterwards back to his for flies and, er, more flies. One kiss for me, one kiss for him, and one for the teapot.

**Gomer:** [*falsetto*] Now you listen to me young Dwarf Molly –

**Molly:** [*baritone*] Hang on a minute . . . shouldn't I be doing the falsetto?

**Gomer:** [*falsetto*] What do you mean . . . oh wait up, you're right . . . [*clears throat*]

**Molly:** [*falsetto*] Chasing the giggling spider children down to spider farm . . .

**Gomer:** [*baritone*] Look you, la, bach, boyo, see, dew, bach, look you, leeks, Rugby football, sheep, curry, beer, male voice choirs, *look* you.

## Ork Sonnets

### I.

Shall I compare thee to an ugh! ugh! ugh!
Thou art more ugh!ular and more *urrh! arrrrh! urh!*
*Gnaargh!* shall *Urghh!* gnash-gnash-gnash—
MANFLESH!! uh! uh! uh!
Arrrgghhhh!
*Aaaaaaarrrrghh!*
*Ugh!!* UGH! hath all too short a UGH!
RAAAAAGGH! WAAAAAARRGH!
Thank you. Gestetnered copies of my selected poems
Are available in the lobby, price three groats.

### II.

You've
got
to
*Fight* the power!
*Fight* the powers of Man!
You've got to *hack* the helmet,
Disem*bowel* the man-warriors—

272

You've
   Got
      To
*Feed* your belly
*Feed* your belly on the carcasses of your enemies.
You've got to *apply* an emollient, perhaps a *fat*-based
   product like lard to the back of your head to stop
   your helmet chafing, also very important, that.

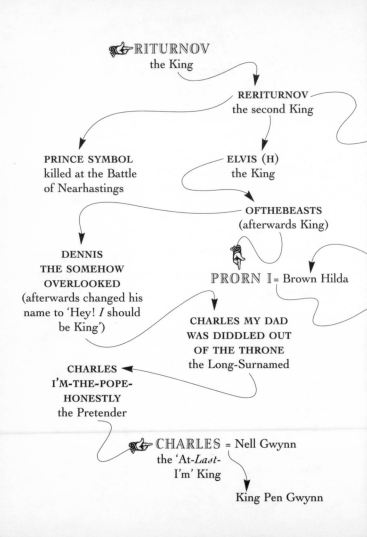

**RITURNOV**
the King

**RERITURNOV**
the second King

**PRINCE SYMBOL**
killed at the Battle
of Nearhastings

**ELVIS (H)**
the King

**OFTHEBEASTS**
(afterwards King)

**DENNIS
THE SOMEHOW
OVERLOOKED**
(afterwards changed his
name to 'Hey! *I* should
be King')

**PRORN I** = Brown Hilda

**CHARLES MY DAD
WAS DIDDLED OUT
OF THE THRONE**
the Long-Surnamed

**CHARLES
I'M-THE-POPE-
HONESTLY**
the Pretender

**CHARLES** = Nell Gwynn
the 'At-*Last*-
I'm' King

King Pen Gwynn

## *The Royal Line of Mannish Monarchs*
### (MOSTLY MEN)

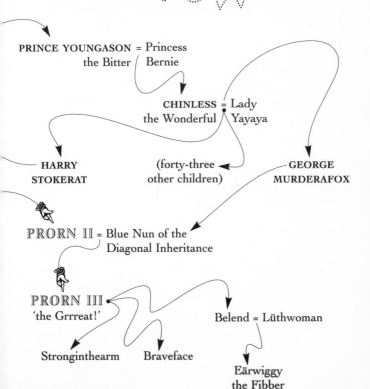

**PRINCE YOUNGASON** = Princess
the Bitter / Bernie

**CHINLESS** = Lady
the Wonderful / Yayaya

**HARRY STOKERAT**

(forty-three other children)

**GEORGE MURDERAFOX**

PRORN II = Blue Nun of the Diagonal Inheritance

PRORN III
'the Grrreat!'

Belend = Lüthwoman

Stronginthearm

Braveface

Eärwiggy the Fibber

# Appendices

# *Note on Pronunciation*

The following note is a guide only, not a comprehensive account of pronunciation in the works of A. R. R. R. Roberts, or any other writer or document, except this document, obviously.

## CONSONANTS

C      always has the value *sea* (as in 'seabiscuit'), except when its value is *kay* (as in 'kayleigh'), unless it is being pronounced *as part of a word*, in which case it is pronounced 'c' (as in 'crunching celery' or 'haecceity').

CH    pronounced as 'c' only with an 'h' after it, *except* when the 'h' part is sort of included in the 'c' part that precedes it, as if instead of two letters there *is* actually only one letter, that happens to have been written down as two letters, perhaps to use up space (as in 'Why is it *always* me who has to write them a postcard? I've nothing to say to them! They're your family after all. Jeesh, I suppose I can just talk about the weather but write in really large letters').

DH      pronounced however you like. No, really.
Whatever takes your fancy. Pronounce it 'q' or 'x' if
you want. No skin off my nose. What do I care how
you sound in the privacy of your own home?

TH      has it ever struck you how *odd* it is that the river
Thames is spelt the way it is? I mean, I'm not a
world expert on word-spell-ology or anything, but
if a word is pronounced Temz, then shouldn't we
write it that way? Or would that make our capital's
river look too much like an Eastern European
bottled lager? These are the sorts of things that
batter into my head as I lie in my bed at night, you
know. The phrase 'keeps me awake at night' is no
mere expression in my case. It's an actual state of
affairs. You ask my wife.

## VOWELS

IE      is always pronounced 'eye-before-ee' *except* when it
is pronounced '*except* after *sea*' (see 'c').

AI      has the value of somebody shot in the stomach
anywhere east of Sri Lanka or west of the
International Date Line.

ERG      has the value of somebody retrieving something
that has rolled under a table, perhaps a bread roll
or some coins, shuffling out backwards on all fours,

not quite gauging the distance properly, and trying to stand up with their head still largely underneath the table.

OU    has the value of somebody with a mouthful of soft-crumb pastry who has inhaled a small crumb of the soft-crumb pastry inadvertently, but can't quite cough properly because their mouth is packed with a sodden mix of flour, butter and saliva.

UW    has the value of somebody caught with a swift backhander that makes their face flip sharply to the left, and propels a tiny stream of dribble horizontally from the corner of their lip.

## ACCENTS

ˋ      means that the letter (but not the whole word) should be pronounced with a German accent.

˙˙     means that the letter (but not the whole word) should be pronounced with a generic 'Asia Minor' or 'Middle Eastern' accent.

~      means that the whole sentence should be spoke in cod-Spanish, and 'olé' added at the end.

ώ      looks a bit testicular, don't you think? Honestly, sometimes I think the people who invent typefaces just get a bit bored from time to time and slip a few in to see if we notice.

ψ     candelabra

Ø     man with bowler hat on at rakish angle

Þ     pregnant lampstand

## *Nonwin Press are proud to announce*

### An exciting new development in Fantasy fiction
### The upgrading of a Fantasy classic

Do you love A. R. R. R. Roberts's *Lowered Off the Rings*?

Yeah? You do?

So do we.

But there's one problem – isn't there? *You* know what we're talking about.

At a mere 1200 pages and three volumes it is simply too short. How can any true Fantasy fan enjoy a book that's over as soon as it begins?

For this reason Nonwin Press has commissioned Fantasy author Roberts Jordan to recast this classic book, to bring it into line with the demands of modern fans of Fantasy fiction.

# Roberts Jordan's
## *The Lord of the Wheels of Time*

A 144-volume rewriting of *Lowered Off the Rings*. Each volume guaranteed *at least* 1000 pages long, with *at least* three maps per volume, lists of characters, glossaries, and a full-colour hyperrealist painted cover art.